"I can't help it if I'm upset," she said

Kelly put her head back on his shoulder.

Ross sighed and handed her his handkerchief. "Why keep tearing yourself up over this guy?" he asked finally. "He isn't worth it."

"I know," she said. "That's why I told Allen tonight I won't see him anymore. I'm not a complete dummy, you know."

"That statement is the first evidence of it I've seen," he murmured.

"You," she said icily, "are the most irritating, annoying, irksome man I have ever met—"

"Without a doubt, you're right." Ross looked down into her bright blue eyes and said huskily, "Oh, hell, Kelly Green."

He kissed her harshly, fiercely. Her first instinct was to break away. Then she thought, there was no reason on earth she should. . . .

Leigh Michaels likes writing romance fiction spiced with humor and a dash of suspense and adventure. She holds a degree in journalism and teaches creative writing in Iowa. She and her husband, a photographer, have two children but include in their family a dog-pound mutt who thinks he's human and a Siamese "aristo-cat," who have both appeared in her books. But when asked if her husband and children have also been characterized, the author pleads the Fifth Amendment.

Books by Leigh Michaels

HARLEQUIN ROMANCE
2657—ON SEPTEMBER HILL
2734—WEDNESDAY'S CHILD
2748—COME NEXT SUMMER
2806—CAPTURE A SHADOW

HARLEQUIN PRESENTS
702—KISS YESTERDAY GOODBYE
811—DEADLINE FOR LOVE
835—DREAMS TO KEEP
876—TOUCH NOT MY HEART
900—LEAVING HOME

Don't miss any of our special offers. Write to us at the following address for information on our newest releases.

Harlequin Reader Service
901 Fuhrmann Blvd., P.O. Box 1397, Buffalo, NY 14240
Canadian address: P.O. Box 603,
Fort Erie, Ont. L2A 5X3

O'Hara's Legacy

Leigh Michaels

Harlequin Books

TORONTO • NEW YORK • LONDON
AMSTERDAM • PARIS • SYDNEY • HAMBURG
STOCKHOLM • ATHENS • TOKYO • MILAN

Original hardcover edition published in 1986
by Mills & Boon Limited

ISBN 0-373-02830-X

Harlequin Romance first edition April 1987

For The Honorable Dick Schlegel
of the Iowa Court of Appeals
Whose legal research set a precedent
that he may come to regret

CHAPTER ONE

IT was the first really warm day of spring, with the daffodils poking their golden crowns through the snow that remained in shaded corners here and there. The soft breeze tugged at Kelly's honey-blonde hair.

She shook her head in wonder at the suddenness of the change. Just last week, it had been bitterly cold, and the snow had still been a foot deep across the land. Just last week, when they had laid Patrick O'Hara to rest on this little hill, it had still been winter.

She stooped beside the freshly-turned earth of the new grave. A few more weeks and they would cover this scar in the earth with sod, and then she could bring some flowers out to plant. And next autumn she'd put daffodil bulbs beside Patrick's grave, so that in the spring . . .

She brushed tears away and tried to smile. He had loved daffodils. She had read the Wordsworth poem to him so many times that she knew it by heart. ' "And then my heart with pleasure fills, and dances with the daffodils",' she murmured. 'I hope there are lots of flowers in heaven for you, Patrick.'

He'd been such a funny old man, she thought. He could bark with anger when something displeased him; he'd been the terror of the nurses on the hospital floor. Kelly had been frantic the first time they'd sent her to sit and read to him. 'I'm a volunteer in this hospital,' she'd protested to the head nurse. 'I'm not a battalion of combat troops!'

Once inside his room, she had been startled by the brightness of his blue eyes. In the wasted, drawn face, they looked like polished sapphires. 'Well, what are you here for?' he had barked. 'Got the palsy, girl? You're shaking like a leaf.'

Kelly had been too startled to answer.

'Can't a man have a little privacy, even in a hospital room?'

Kelly had gathered her scattered courage. 'Is that why you're so nasty? Every patient they've brought in to share your room has asked to be moved within a day.'

He had stared at her for a long moment, and his eyes had sharpened to daggers. Kelly had stood her ground, trying to stop her knees from shaking.

Then, abruptly, he had started to laugh. It was a creaky, rusty sound, as if he didn't do it much. 'Well, it works,' he'd said. 'I get a private room, without paying for it. Come in, come in. What's your name?'

'Kelly Sheridan.' She had found her way to the chair beside his bed, not taking her eyes off him.

'With two good Irish names like those, you ought to be a redhead.' It had sounded like an order.

'I don't plan to dye my hair to please you, Mr O'Hara.' Then she had swallowed hard at her own impertinence.

He had loved it. In the next two weeks, as his health fluctuated and he lay in the hospital bed, Kelly had spent hours reading to him, and listening to him talk about his cat and the old days. He wanted to go home, he said, but there was no one to take care of him there. And they both knew, though they never said it, that for Patrick O'Hara, going home was a dream that would never come true.

The day they had moved him to the nursing home had been the worst, she thought. He had clung to her hand, trying to thank her, and for the first time she had seen the gleam of tears in the old man's eyes.

She hadn't said anything to him then, but when she'd turned up at the nursing home the next day, with his favourite book in her hand he had cried, unashamedly.

They said he'd died of congestive heart failure, but Kelly knew better. He'd made up his mind that he'd rather be here, on the quiet hill surrounded by warm breezes and daffodils, than lying in that hard mechanical bed, with life support systems standing by. He had quietly resigned himself from life, and set about dying . . .

'What happened to your cat, Patrick?' she asked quietly. 'You never told me where you left Rapunzel. Or did she die, too, and you just didn't want to admit that she was gone?'

She brushed a hand across the small marble headstone. The date of death had not yet been chiselled in; she hoped that someone would take care of that. He'd had a family, somewhere, but he'd never talked about his relatives. At least, she assumed he'd had a family. There had been a woman at his funeral, one Kelly had never seen before. A white-haired, distinguished woman in her fifties—a sister, perhaps? Or an old love? Kelly hadn't wanted to intrude; she had stayed on the fringe of the small group of people and left as soon as the ceremonies were over. After all, she had no real place there, among Patrick's people.

She rubbed a finger across the slick surface of the stone. Well, if the date remained uncarved, she'd take care of it herself, just as soon as she had a few extra dollars to pay for the work.

At any rate, she told herself firmly, it was time to stop sitting about the cemetery and get over to the hospital. Even if she was only a volunteer, the nurses still depended on her to show up on time. She picked her bicycle up from the gravelled path and pedalled off, trying to make up for lost time.

Patrick would have smiled at that, too, she thought. He often had chided her for putting things off till the last moment and then arriving at a dead run. 'Kelly Green,' he would say, 'you're going to give yourself a nervous breakdown, doing that.' And Kelly would smile at the nickname, and promise to plan ahead next time.

She was still pinning her hair up into a roll at the nape of her neck when the elevator delivered her to the nurses' station.

The dark-haired young woman at the desk looked up from a patient's chart with a smile. 'I knew that had to be you, Kelly,' she said. 'The elevator only has that particular hurried wheeze when you're on board.'

'Thanks a lot, Cathy.' She put the last hairpin in and reached into a closet for the red jacket that marked her as an official volunteer. 'Anything special to be done today?'

'Oh, Mrs Ainsley's being a pill. She's just at the awkward stage—enough better that she doesn't need a nurse at her fingertips every moment, but still feeling too awful to entertain herself.'

'I can't wait,' Kelly said. She'd tried to keep Mrs Ainsley company before.

'And one of the florists dumped off a whole truckload of cut flowers. Why, I have no idea. But if you'd like to practise your flower arranging——'

'Can I do that instead of sitting with Mrs Ainsley?' Kelly asked, bright-eyed.

'Sorry. The head nurse said the sour comes with the sweet. Oh, you had a phone call, too. He wanted you to call back.' She flipped through a stack of message slips.

'He?' Kelly questioned. She took the slip of paper with a frown. Who would be calling her at the hospital?

'It wasn't your beloved Allen,' Cathy said. 'I've talked to him so often I'd recognise him in my sleep. Here it is.'

Kelly ignored her. Cathy had never liked Allen. 'Roger Bradford, of Bradford and Parrish? That's Allen's father's law firm. I wonder——'

'Well, why don't you call, so we can all stop wondering?' Cathy recommended, and set the phone on to the counter where Kelly could reach it. 'Maybe it's a job offer.'

'I couldn't be so lucky. I've gone six months now without a paying job—wouldn't you think something would turn up soon?'

'That's one thing about nursing,' Cathy mused. 'The

pay isn't great, but there are always jobs.'

'I'm just about to go back to school.'

Cathy grinned. 'What's the matter? Are you afraid to leave Allen alone over in the College of Law?'

'Not at all. I'm not the jealous sort. But I'm thinking of taking up something useful.' She paused, and then added drily, 'Welding, maybe.'

A dulcet voice on the other end of the line reported that she had reached Bradford and Parrish, Attorneys at Law.

'Kelly Sheridan returning Mr Bradford's call,' she said crisply.

'Very good. Maybe you could be a secretary,' Cathy applauded.

Kelly cupped her hand over the phone. 'You know I've tried. Do you know how many secretaries are out of work in this town? Good ones, too—that type and file and everything.'

'Miss Sheridan?' It was a new voice, thin and reedy. She hoped that Roger Bradford didn't spend much time in a courtroom; he'd put all the jurors to sleep.

'Did you know Mr Patrick O'Hara?' The man's question was sharp, and for a moment Kelly panicked.

'Of course I did,' she said.

'And did you take it upon yourself to visit him in his last illness, and did he even at times refer to you as—let me see . . .'

'Kelly Green,' she supplied irritably. She didn't like the tone of these questions, she told herself. Surely there was no law against visiting an old man in a nursing home!

'Miss Green—I'm so sorry, I meant to say Miss Sheridan—could you come to my office this afternoon?'

'Give me one good reason,' she said, a little tartly.

Roger Bradford laughed. 'I'm sorry if it sounded like an inquisition,' he said. 'It's just that Patrick wasn't very clear about precisely who you were, and I've been looking for you for a couple of days. We'll be reading the will this afternoon, you see.'

Kelly blinked. 'Patrick named me in his will?'

'He probably left you the cat,' Cathy muttered under her breath.

'I'm not at liberty to discuss it further at this time,' the lawyer said smoothly. 'Shall we say, four o'clock?'

'I'll be there.' She put the phone down, feeling a little dazed. 'Patrick——'

'I heard,' Cathy said. 'I would never have dreamed that he owned anything of value.'

'Oh, I don't know. He was a wise old guy when it came to saving money.' She smiled a little, thinking about Patrick's never-fail method to save the cost of a private room.

'Whatever it is, I hope it's worth all the time you spent with him.'

'Cathy!' She was horrified. 'I visited him because I liked to, not because I hoped he'd leave me something.'

'Good. Because you'll probably end up with his complete set of William Wordsworth.'

'Don't forget the cat,' Kelly recommended, and went off with a lighter heart to read to Mrs Ainsley.

The smell of spring had even reached downtown, and the small trees that lined the city streets seemed to have an aura of hazy green. In another two weeks, the leaves would have burst forth in full glory, but right now there was only promise. The gutters were running full with melting snow as the last of winter disappeared. If she closed her eyes, she thought, she could pretend to be out in the country, beside a babbling brook.

She had never been to the law office before. Allen was just starting law school, and in another couple of years he would join his father's firm, as soon as he passed his bar exams. He'd practically grown up in that office, but to Kelly it was a new world. Something of a scary one at that, she thought, especially since Allen's father thought that a first-year law student was far too young to commit himself to marriage. She wasn't even really sure that Allen had told his parents much about her.

There was plenty of time for that, she thought. They were in love, but they weren't foolish enough to rush into anything. They had both seen young marriages crack under the strain when the wife worked in order to put the husband through school, or when the new couple had to depend on their parents for support. No, it made more sense to wait till Allen was finished at school. Then they could be married, have their own apartment, begin their new lives ...

Frankly, Kelly told herself, she was glad that it was Roger Bradford, and not John Parrish, that she would be seeing today. She didn't want to complicate things for herself and Allen.

Absorbed in her thoughts, she almost missed the entrance to the car park, and at the last minute she had to swerve her bicycle across two lanes of traffic. Brakes squealed behind her, and the bumper of a dark-blue sports car seemed to brush against her back wheel as she started her turn. A man's head popped out of the car window, and he yelled across the street, 'You ought to be locked up!'

She shrugged, trying to look suitably apologetic. It hadn't been exactly polite of her to turn without signalling, but there was no reason for him to be so upset, she thought. After all, he'd been following her too closely, or he wouldn't have had any trouble stopping. He must be a Type A personality, she diagnosed. Nervous, fretful, intense; a perfectionist who was always trying to stay five minutes ahead of himself. The kind who would die of a heart attack before he was fifty.

But nice-looking, she added to herself. His hair had gleamed black in the sunshine, his face showed a nice, even winter tan, and from that brief glimpse of his broad shoulders she could tell that he was powerfully built. Too bad that such a handsome man has to be afflicted with an abrasive personality, she thought; I'll bet if he'd just slow down and smile he'd be charming.

She locked her bike up carefully on the pavement and entered the quiet, elegant office suite. Patrick would have applauded, she thought as she checked her watch. She was two minutes early.

A heavy door across the reception room opened, and Allen came out. He looked astonished at the sight of Kelly, and came quickly across the room to her. 'What are you doing here?' he demanded in a conspiratorial whisper. 'It's not very smart of you, that's sure. If Dad finds out you're sitting here waiting for me——'

'Don't tell him,' Kelly recommended, 'because I'm not waiting for you. I didn't expect to see you here.'

'I'm doing some research for Dad. If you're not here because of me, then why——?'

A tall, bald-headed man had opened another office door, and now he said, 'Miss Sheridan? Come in, please.' Allen looked astounded as she walked across to Roger Bradford's office. The attorney indicated a chair and told the secretary to bring her a cup of coffee.

After a few minutes of small talk, he saw her glance at her wristwatch. 'I'm sorry to delay you, Miss Sheridan,' he said smoothly. 'We must wait for Patrick's cousin to arrive before we can read the will.'

The woman at the funeral, Kelly thought, and congratulated herself. 'Patrick never talked about his relatives,' she said. 'Were they close?'

'Well, as far as that goes——' Mr Bradford caught himself before he let a confidence slip. 'He's late now, and I can't think what's keeping him. It isn't like him.'

He? she wondered. Well, it would soon be explained.

'How did you get to know Patrick, Miss Sheridan? Oh, yes, I remember now—at the hospital. His last illness was really an extended affair, you know. He hadn't been well for over a year.'

It sounded like some kind of warning. Kelly wondered why, and then dismissed it. It was probably just the lawyer's way—conservative to a fault.

What would Patrick's cousin be like, she wondered, and couldn't help but picture Patrick himself, white-haired, gentle, but in good health, as he must have looked five years ago. 'Is his name O'Hara too?' she asked. 'The cousin, I mean?'

'No. His name is Clayton. Ross Clayton.' He looked at her as if he expected her to applaud.

There was a tap on the door, and Kelly sat up straight, wanting to make a good impression. Then a very good-looking, very irritable young man came into the office, and she would have given anything to be able to turn herself into a puff of smoke and vanish out the window. This was Patrick's cousin? she thought, in disbelief.

'Sorry to be late, Mr Bradford,' the man said briefly, 'but a dumb bicyclist did a U-turn in front of me, and by the time I recovered from that I'd missed the car park and had to go clear around.'

I was right, Kelly thought. He does have a charming smile. Then he saw her, and the smile died.

'You!' he said. His eyes were blue, and right now they were as hard as the sapphires they looked like. He had Patrick's eyes, she thought—but Patrick had never looked at her like this.

'It was not a U-turn, it was a left turn,' Kelly snapped, and then bit her tongue.

'I don't give a darn if you'd suddenly decided to fly to the moon, it was a damn fool thing to do. You could have killed yourself!'

'Not to mention scratching your bumper,' she said sweetly.

'It's probably worth more than you are. So you're Uncle Patrick's little——'

She gritted her teeth. 'You'd better be careful what you say,' she warned. 'There's an attorney present, and he'd make a wonderful witness at a slander trial!'

He grinned evilly, and then finished his sentence. 'Friend,' he said, with awful emphasis. 'But tell me,

Miss Sheridan—why did you jump to the conclusion that I was going to say anything unflattering about you?'

'Children, children!' Roger Bradford said. They both stared at him. He seemed to suddenly hear what he had said, and he coloured 'Well, you sound like kids,' he said mildly. 'If you'd stop this infernal bickering, we could get down to the business at hand.'

'This is a waste of time, you know,' Ross Clayton said clearly. 'He never owned anything more than the clothes on his back——'

The attorney cut him off in mid-sentence. 'Good,' he said. 'Then since we're all in agreement about the importance of reading the will, let's not drag it out any longer than necessary.'

Kelly would have liked to applaud. Instead, she settled back in her chair and said sweetly, 'I haven't had the—pleasure—of being introduced, Mr Bradford.'

The young man fired a look of disgust at her, and then said, curtly, 'Let's get on with this.'

The attorney reached into a drawer.

Kelly continued, 'Aren't you a bit young to be a cousin to Patrick O'Hara?'

Mr Bradford cleared his throat.

Kelly favoured him with a smile and said, apologetically, to Ross Clayton, 'I just wanted to get it clear in my mind, you see. Mr Bradford said you were cousins, but then you called him Uncle Patrick. Patrick never mentioned you at all, and—well, I'm sorry, but you were a bit of an unpleasant surprise.'

'Likewise, Miss Sheridan.'

She swallowed hard at the loathing in his voice, and then went on. 'I was just puzzled, you see,' she confided.

He was beginning to look like a thundercloud. 'My mother and Patrick were first cousins,' he said. 'I always considered him my uncle because he was so much older. Now if that satisfies your curiosity, can we get on with the reading of the will?'

The attorney spread the sheaf of paper out on his desk blotter and took a deep breath.

Kelly shifted in her chair and murmured, 'If you're so certain, Mr Clayton, that Patrick didn't have anything worth leaving, then why are you so upset at the idea that he might have left some of it to me?'

Mr Bradford put his head down in his hands.

Ross Clayton looked as if he'd swallowed something unpleasant.

'That's the only thing that was puzzling me, you see,' Kelly said politely.

There was a brief silence. Mr Bradford looked up warily, as if to see if it was safe to come out. 'May I go ahead now?' he asked.

Kelly waved a hand, disclaiming any desire to hold up the proceedings.

'Just a minute,' Ross Clayton said. 'I want to answer that, before I've heard what Patrick put in that will.'

Mr Bradford made a gesture, started to protest, then refolded the will and put it back in the drawer. 'Whenever you're ready, let me know,' he said, his voice resigned.

'I had no idea,' Ross said, 'that there was a young woman hanging about Uncle Patrick at the nursing home.'

'Which was more than you were doing,' Kelly pointed out. 'Hanging about, I mean. You never spent any time with him.'

He shot a look of animosity toward her. 'I don't live here in town,' he said, 'and why I'm explaining this to you is more than I can understand.'

'Oh,' she said, on a note of discovery. 'That explains why I didn't see you at his funeral.'

'I've been out on the West Coast finishing up a job, and it prevented me from—— Look, this is ridiculous! I don't have to explain anything to you!'

'That's right,' she said sweetly. 'And likewise, I don't have to give you any excuses either. I'd be delighted to have something of Patrick's, because he was a sweet little old man, and I miss him very much.'

'Yes, I'm sure you do,' he said, his voice heavy with irony. 'It's unfortunate for you, Miss Sheridan, that you didn't stake out your territory a little more clearly. Or did Patrick die just a little sooner than you expected?'

'I think this has gone far enough,' Mr Bradford said firmly. They both looked at him in astonishment, as if he'd suddenly appeared from nowhere. 'If you two are going to come to blows, would you kindly do so out on the street—and not in my office?' He took the will from the drawer again. 'I'll skip the preliminaries, because there is no doubt, of course, that Patrick was of sound mind when he wrote this.'

'That remains to be seen,' Ross muttered.

The document was pages thick. There were an awful lot of words there to dispose of nothing, Kelly thought, and caught herself crossing her fingers. After six months without a job, anything Patrick might have left her would be like manna from heaven. Even a hundred dollars would make a tremendous difference in how she was living right now.

Then she lectured herself. Don't be grasping, she told herself sternly. Blood is thicker than water, and if Patrick had owned anything important, he would surely want his family to have it, not her. He had no doubt left her some token, but it probably wasn't cash. She rather suspected that Ross Clayton was right, that Patrick had owned very little.

'To Kelly Sheridan, I leave my complete set of A. Conan Doyle——'

'I'm a Sherlock Holmes fan,' Kelly murmured to Ross Clayton.

Mr Bradford pressed on, allowing no time for an answer. 'And my leather-bound William Wordsworth, in the hope that she will not forget the pleasure I found in the hours she read to me.'

Ross Clayton grinned. 'You can't win them all,' he said under his breath. 'My condolences, Miss Sheridan.'

Kelly released the breath she'd been holding. Well, it was all she had expected, and it was nice of Patrick to have thought of her at all, she told herself.

'Also my mother's silver tea service,' Mr Bradford said smoothly, and Ross frowned.

A silver tea service? Kelly thought. That was the most impractical thing she'd ever heard of—but nice of Patrick for all that. Some day she and Allen would have a house to put it in . . .

'To Ross Clayton, I leave all of the family photographs which I have collected through the years . . .'

Kelly couldn't help it. She tried to smother the laugh, but it came out as something between a gulp and a sneeze.

Mr Bradford sent her a quelling look. 'In the hope that he will continue to preserve them for future generations.'

'There aren't going to be any future generations,' Ross growled.

'Understandable,' Kelly said. 'What woman would have you?'

Mr Bradford put the document down. 'Would you two be serious?' he asked coldly, and continued before they could set off another argument. 'Also the family Bible——'

Ross Clayton put his hand over his eyes. 'I came all the way out here to get the family Bible?' he muttered to no one in particular.

Kelly offered helpfully, 'Perhaps Patrick thought it would benefit you to——'

Mr Bradford raised his voice and kept reading. 'And my mother's set of bone china.'

'Bone china? How am I supposed to get that home? I'll trade you for the silver service,' he offered Kelly.

Mr Bradford was starting to shout. 'The remainder of my property, both real and personal, I leave——'

Kelly said, suddenly, 'What about the cat?'

Mr Bradford pulled a handkerchief from his pocket and wiped his perspiring forehead. He seemed to be debating with himself, but curiosity won out. 'What cat?' he asked warily.

'Patrick's cat,' Kelly explained patiently. 'Rapunzel.'

'Patrick had a cat named Rapunzel?' Ross Clayton sounded as if he thought she'd finally lost her mind completely.

'Of course,' Kelly said, and added demurely, 'he called her that because she'd go out now and then and—umm, let her hair down, and then she'd come home to have her kittens.'

Mr Bradford started to choke. 'Patrick made no specific provision for a cat, Miss Sheridan.'

'Oh. Well, you see, I can't understand that. Patrick was very fond of Rapunzel, and——'

'You can have Rapunzel!' Ross Clayton shouted. 'Now can we finish this?'

The other two looked at him in astonishment. Then Mr Bradford picked up the will again, pushed his glasses up on the bridge of his nose, and read, very rapidly, 'The remainder of my property, both real and personal, I leave to the aforementioned Kelly Sheridan——'

'What?' Ross Clayton shouted.

'and to the aforementioned Ross Clayton as tenants in common, share and share alike.' Mr Bradford stopped, breathless, and reached for his handkerchief again. 'There. That's all of it.'

There was a long moment of silence.

'What property are we talking about?' Ross asked genially.

'The main thing is the bookstore, of course,' Mr Bradford laid his glasses aside. 'There is a little money in a savings account, and——'

'I didn't know Patrick owned a bookstore,' Kelly murmured.

'I'll just bet you didn't,' Ross Clayton said. 'Well, Mr Bradford, that's simple enough. Sell the bookstore and mail me my money. Now if that's all——' He was on his feet.

'That's not all,' Kelly objected. 'What if I want to keep the bookstore? I'd at least like to look at it——'

'Then look at it. But my half is for sale.'

Mr Bradford sighed. 'I'm afraid it really isn't that simple, Ross,' he said, 'for a couple of reasons. First is that Patrick had been ill for a long time, and the store had correspondingly not been kept up to standard. Besides that, once the owner of a business dies, the good will that he has built up dies too.'

'What does that mean?' Kelly asked.

'Basically, it means that the bookstore is only worth what the stock will bring. Since Patrick dealt mainly in used books, it won't be much—a couple of thousand dollars, perhaps. Besides that, Patrick had a lease on the building through to the end of the summer, and the costs of that will have to be satisfied before the estate can be settled.'

'So sell off the stock and settle the debts,' Ross Clayton said. 'That's your job, Mr Bradford.'

'I think it would be fun to run a bookstore,' Kelly said obstinately. 'I want to keep my share.'

The attorney picked up his glasses again and perched them on the end of his nose. 'And then, of course, there's the biggest problem of all,' he said.

'And that is?' Kelly asked warily.

'The will names you as tenants in common. That means, basically, that neither one of you can act without the other's permission.'

There was a moment of shocked silence. 'Do you mean we have to agree on everything?' Ross Clayton said. There was an anguished note in his voice.

'That's what I mean,' Mr Bradford said sadly. 'That is exactly what I mean.'

CHAPTER TWO

Ross Clayton sat down heavily in his chair. 'That tears it,' he said. 'If Patrick had set out to create an impossible situation, he couldn't have done a better job.'

'Now that I'll agree with.' Kelly looked at him with distaste.

Mr Bradford said plaintively, 'If I might give you some advice?'

They both looked at him as if they'd forgotten he was there.

'Why did Patrick do this?' Ross Clayton complained. 'If he was trying to turn me into a crusty old bookstore owner like himself——'

'Well, as for being crusty,' Kelly began.

'He had no such intention, Ross,' Mr Bradford said. 'If he'd wanted to force you to run the bookstore, he'd have put a provision in the will saying that you couldn't sell it.'

Ross Clayton didn't look convinced.

'It's probably a waste of breath to talk to you two,' Mr Bradford added, almost to himself, 'but I'll try. Patrick wanted you each to have a reasonable amount of money when you were finished, but he didn't realise how much his illness had hurt the value of his business. The only way I see for you to profit is for you to keep the store intact——'

Kelly stifled the urge to stick out her tongue at Ross Clayton. 'See?' she said.

Mr Bradford sighed. 'Hire someone to run it for a year or so, and put the profits back into the store. Once the business is built up, sell it. You'd have a tidy profit.'

They were silent. It made sense, Kelly thought, except

for one thing—she wasn't interested in selling at any time.

'The only alternative,' he went on, 'if you can't agree, is for one of you to bring suit against the other one, asking for an accounting of the assets of the business and an equal division—a partition action. All that accomplishes is that you'll sell out anyway, and the costs will eat up any profit there might have been. What it comes down to is that you have to agree to something, and soon.' He reached into a bottom desk drawer and tossed a key on to the blotter. 'Why don't you go to look the property over?' he suggested wearily. 'Perhaps after you see it, you can come to some sort of agreement.'

'I wouldn't bet on it,' Ross Clayton said under his breath. He turned to Kelly. 'Why do you want to own a bookstore?'

'Why not? It's as good a job as most.'

'Oh, now you intend to run it?'

'It's better than a lot of things I've done.' She saw him start to smile, and added, trying to keep her composure, 'Such as washing dishes in the student union cafeteria.'

'I see. That experience is a real qualification for running a retail business.'

'I happen to have a degree in literature.' She reached for the key. He grabbed for the ring, and she held it out of his reach. 'Not so fast,' she warned. 'If we're going at all, we stay together.'

'Let me know what you decide,' Mr Bradford said.

Kelly took a look back from the doorway, and saw him start to sag thankfully in his chair.

'What do you do, anyway?' she asked Ross Clayton.

'What business is it of yours?'

'I think I should know before I take you on as a partner.'

Allen was walking across the reception room with a stack of law books. He stopped short at the sound of Kelly's voice. 'Partner?' he said.

'Later, Allen,' Kelly said. 'Call me tonight and I'll explain it all.'

'Is he your boyfriend?' Ross Clayton asked as they reached the car park. 'What's he doing in the attorney's office?'

'Why are you asking?' she said sweetly. 'Shall we meet at the store? Where is it, by the way?'

'You don't know?'

'Cross my heart. Patrick never breathed a word about it.'

He eyed the key in her hand and said, reluctantly, 'Leave the bike here. I'll bring you back.'

She debated that one for a moment, and decided that she didn't have much choice. Even though she had possession of the key, she wouldn't put a great deal of trust in any address he gave her. So she meekly got into his car. 'I just want to remind you,' she murmured, 'that if I mysteriously disappear, Mr Bradford will have a pretty good idea of what happened to me.'

His eyes seemed to smoulder, and then the car shot out of the car park with far more force than was necessary.

The bookstore was just a few blocks away, but it was like travelling into another town, or another time. This section had been left behind when the downtown area had been rebuilt and modernised. The storefronts were dilapidated, and many of the buildings were empty. It was a part of town that Kelly had never explored.

Ross Clayton parked the sports car in front of a two-storey brick building. Dusty bay windows on both floors were the only distinguishing architectural feature; in every other way the structure was like thousands of retail stores built at the turn of the century.

'At least it looks structurally sound,' Kelly murmured.

'That figures. We don't own the building, just the business.' He looked into the bay windows, where books were piled haphazardly. Peeling paint on the glass spelled out the bookstore's name. 'The Bookworm?' Ross said. 'That sounds like Patrick.'

'Oh, stop grumbling,' she ordered. 'Do you ever look at the positive side of anything?'

'At the moment, Miss Sheridan, it's hard for me to believe that this problem has a positive side. May I have the key, please?'

'If you don't mind,' she said sweetly, 'I'll do it myself.'

The lock clicked and the door swung open with an eerie creak. The air inside was stale, as if it had been trapped there all winter, and dust lay thick over the counters and the rows and rows of shelves. Books were piled on the shelves, on the floor, on the countertops, crammed in any way they would fit. What a job it would be to clean out this mess, Kelly thought. The late afternoon gloom was casting long shadows across the floor, leaving much of the shop in darkness. She stopped just inside the doorway to let her eyes become accustomed to the dusk.

Once she could see more clearly, though, she realised that the little store had considerable charm. There was a fireplace along one wall, with a couple of rocking chairs in front of it, and almost in the centre of the store was a spiral staircase. She wondered what was upstairs. Stockrooms, perhaps? More books? She sighed. There must be some treasures here, she thought, but finding them in the middle of all the junk would be the hard part.

Nevertheless, she was going to have to try. This was like an answer to prayer—she had been frantically seeking a job, and here was one handed to her. One she was ideally suited for, at that, with her tastes and training. She turned a little, to send a curious glance towards Ross Clayton. He wouldn't be easy to convince, but somehow she must make him understand how important it was to her that the bookstore opened again.

He had stopped by the door, as if horrified by what he was seeing. And it was a shock, Kelly had to admit.

It wasn't quite the neat little storefront with tidy racks of best-sellers that she had hoped for. But it could be made to be profitable again, she was certain.

She took a deep breath and started towards him. She was beginning to regret the quick tongue that had made her say all those nasty things to him; now she would have to patch up the damage she'd done, and it wouldn't be easy. He wasn't the kind to take lightly to flattery . . .

The lights flashed on, almost blinding her, and she flung up a hand.

'What the devil——' Ross Clayton exclaimed.

'The very thing I was asking meself,' came a creaky voice from the spiral staircase.

For a split second, Kelly thought, It's Patrick. We've not only got a bookstore, but a ghost——

But in the next moment, she knew better. So far as she knew, no ghost had ever materialised carrying a shotgun, and that certainly was no illusion. The distinctive sound of the gun being cocked echoed through the store.

'So you've got ten seconds to tell me what you're doing in me store,' said the Nemesis on the staircase.

'But it's our——' Kelly began.

'Kelly, for the love of heaven, shut up for once in your life and let me explain it!' Ross Clayton said under his breath.

'So start talking,' she ordered. Her teeth were beginning to chatter. She had no idea what kind of a shot the old man was, but even crouched on the stairs, he could hardly miss them with that gun.

Ross was already explaining the whole chain of circumstances. 'Mr Bradford must have forgotten to call you and tell you we were coming over,' he finished, on a hopeful note.

The old man was quiet for a moment, assessing the story, the gun trained unwaveringly on them. Kelly's eye was caught by another shadow flitting down the spiral stairs, and she called, 'That's Rapunzel!'

She started toward the cat, and Ross Clayton's hand locked on her arm and pulled her back against him with the force of a collision. 'Will you stay still, you little idiot!' he hissed in her ear. 'You'll get us both killed!'

He was right, of course. What a stupid thing to do, with a gun threatening them——

'But she'll get away!' she wailed, watching as the cat leaped up on to the ledge under one of the bay windows and pushed against a panel. It swung silently on hinges and she vanished into the dusk.

Ross Clayton's arms tightened around her, as if he was afraid that she'd follow the cat. Kelly didn't bother to struggle. It was obvious that he wasn't going to let go, and she could never break free from that grip. The man must lift weights, she thought resentfully.

'So you know Rapunzel, do you?' the man on the stairs said.

'Well, not personally,' Kelly said. 'Patrick didn't mention her in his will, and I've been worried about her.'

There was another hesitation, and then the old man lowered the gun to his side and came slowly down the stairs, limping a little. 'Joe Keswick is my name,' he said. 'I own the building. Can't blame me for wondering about intruders, now, can you?'

'Of course not,' Kelly said. 'There are an awful lot of burglaries around here these days . . .' She felt as if she was babbling.

Ross Clayton was still eyeing the gun. 'I'd feel a lot more comfortable if you'd put that thing down,' he said finally.

'What? This?' Joe Keswick looked at the weapon, and then at them, and laughed. ''Tain't loaded,' he confided. 'Man can get in a lot of trouble in this town, waving a loaded gun around.'

'I see,' Ross Clayton murmured.

'What can I help you with? Came to inspect the store, hmm? I imagine you'll be selling out?'

'No,' Kelly said definitely.

'Yes,' Ross Clayton said at the same moment.

Joe Keswick looked a little bemused, then he shrugged it off. 'Any questions you have, just ask 'em. I've owned this building fifty years. Not much I don't know about it. Patrick's lease includes the apartment upstairs, too, if you'd like to look it over.'

'An apartment?' Kelly's eyes were glowing. She turned to Ross Clayton. 'It would cut my living expenses to almost nothing,' she said eagerly.

'It might—but it isn't going to,' he returned briefly.

'Oh, be a sport. At least let's look.' She followed the wizened little man up the spiral stairs. In the hallway above, she counted four doors, each with a number on it. She looked at Joe with puzzlement in her eyes. 'One apartment, you said?'

'Four, actually. I have one of the back ones. The other is empty just now—college kid had it, and I had to ask him to move. You know how kids are these days.' Then he seemed to realise that she wasn't much more than a kid herself, and looked a little doubtful. 'Patrick had the front two. Said he needed plenty of space. He even put some of his things up in the attic. Never saw one old man with so much stuff in my life.'

'The apartments are connected?'

'He just cut a door between them.' He chuckled. 'I told him he had to leave both kitchens, so he'd use one till the dishes was all dirty, then he'd switch to the other. Then he'd clean 'em both up and start over.'

Kelly's stomach flinched a little at that.

Ross Clayton smothered a smile and said, with false concern, 'Why, Miss Sheridan, you're turning pale green.'

But when Joe Keswick pushed the door open, she saw that the apartment wasn't as bad as she had expected. It was basically one big room, with the kitchen area closest to the door, and the living room fronting on the street. Off to the side was a small bedroom and bathroom. The rooms were full, of course. There was little furniture, but books were everywhere—spilling off shelves, piled on tables, stacked on the floor. 'The place needs a good spring-cleaning,' she said to herself.

'Yeah,' Joe Keswick conceded. 'Patrick didn't care much about dust.'

'That's apparent.' She walked across to the bay window and perched on the windowseat. Some frilly curtains, she was thinking, and a bit of paint——

But unless she could persuade Ross Clayton to go along with her plan, there was no point in even dreaming of a new decorating scheme. Heaven knew, there wouldn't be money to do anything, anyway . . .

He was looking around as if he had been trapped in a museum he didn't care for. 'Does this door lead to the other apartment?' he asked.

Joe Keswick nodded. 'He wanted me to take out the wall entirely, but I never got round to it. Would have been easy enough, I suppose. The whole second floor used to be just a storeroom.'

'Yes, I see.' They all trooped in to look. The second apartment was a mirror of the first, but the living room was piled almost to the ceiling with books.

'I see he'd given up on building shelves,' Kelly said.

Ross Clayton looked at his watch. 'I hate to break up the party,' he said, 'but it's getting late. Anything else you want to look at tonight?'

'No, I've seen enough.' Kelly was thoughtful.

'So have I. More than enough.'

'Thank you, Mr Keswick.' Kelly turned on the charm. If she was going to make a go of this store, she'd better stay on good terms with the landlord.

Ross Clayton heaved a sigh of relief as he started the car. 'Well, I'm glad that's over,' he said. 'We'll have Mr Bradford hire someone to arrange an auction of all of Patrick's things. It will pay for the rest of the lease, I'm sure, and perhaps even leave us with a profit. Some of that furniture wasn't in bad shape.'

Kelly let the silence go on for a brief moment. Then she said, 'What do you mean, auction Patrick's things? I haven't changed my mind.'

'You said you'd seen enough——'

'Yes. Enough to know that the store can be turned around, and that I want to have a try at it.'

He groaned. 'Miss Sheridan, really——'

'You called me Kelly when Mr Keswick was holding the gun on us,' she reminded.

'I did? Well, you should be thankful I didn't call you something worse than that. Danger does strange things to people Now as far as the bookstore goes——'

'May I call you Ross?'

He sighed. 'I suppose I can't stop you. Why on earth——'

'Do you have a date tonight?'

'What is this, a proposition?'

Kelly tried not to turn red. 'No. I just thought that if you hadn't made plans for the evening, perhaps we could have dinner and discuss this in a civilised manner.'

'We can discuss it with Mr Bradford in the morning.'

'At his regular rate per hour,' Kelly pointed out. 'And it's all coming out of Patrick's estate. I can't think why we didn't realise what that argument was costing per minute this afternoon.'

'That's true,' he admitted, and looked at her with what might have been a hint of respect in his eyes.

Kelly pressed her advantage. 'There's a lovely little Italian place that serves fifty different kinds of spaghetti. Shall we try it?'

There was a long silence.

'I'll buy,' she added tartly.

He grinned. 'What the heck.'

Mamma Mia's was located in a old converted house just off campus. It was as busy as always, but Mamma found them a table in a corner of what had been the formal living-room, next to the fireplace. As she handed them menus, she looked approvingly at Ross, and then winked at Kelly as if to say, 'Now you've found a man, my girl.'

Sorry, Mamma, Kelly thought. The very idea that Mamma thought she was romantically interested in Ross Clayton was enough to send chills up her spine. She shrugged off the thought and turned to her menu.

'I can recommend the mushroom sauce,' she said. 'Or the marinara, or the Italian sausage.'

'Sausage with spaghetti?' he asked.

'Of course. It's excellent. I can't vouch for the sauce with chicken livers, because I've never eaten it, but I'm sure that Mamma——'

He shuddered. 'You don't have to go through the whole menu. I'll stick to the kind with meatballs, thanks.'

'And some wine, perhaps?'

'Not for me. Something tells me I'm going to need a clear head before the night is over.'

She refused to let the jab disturb her. 'I think the only sensible thing for us to do is to take Mr Bradford's advice,' she said. 'But instead of hiring somebody, which would cost us a great deal, I'll run the store. Just a minute,' she said, as he started to speak. 'It won't have to make any difference to you at all. The way I look at it is this—you can sell out now, or you can let me have a stab at it. It'll take the best part of six months to sell everything, unless you just want to give it all away. In the same six months I'll bet I can have the place on its feet again. You've got nothing to lose.'

'When you put it that way, you make a frightening kind of sense,' he said, and looked suspiciously at his water glass. 'What did they put in this stuff? It must have been something mind-altering, to make me sit here and listen to you.'

'Come on, Ross. Why not give me a chance?'

'Because I don't trust you. Who's to say you won't drain any profit out before I ever see the balance sheets?'

'If you're worried about profit, you certainly won't see any by selling now.'

'At least I'd be done with it,' he pointed out.

'And unless you have an auction in the next few days, you won't know if I'm being fair anyway,' she added. 'Once you go back home, I can do whatever I like—and not even Mr Bradford would know if I don't account for all of the money.'

'You assured me you'd be fair.'

'Only if you give me a chance. Because I'm not going to give in,' she announced with finality. 'You'll have to sue me for—what did Mr Bradford call it? Partition?'

'It'll cost you money too,' he warned.

'I don't care.' She knew that she sounded like a stubborn child, but she felt as if she were fighting for her life.

Mamma put steaming plates in front of them and slapped a basket of hot bread down in the centre of the table. 'Such a serious discussion,' she said. 'It's not good for the digestion to be so gloomy at meals. Laugh a little, have a good time! Two young people, what troubles do you have?' She was gone before there was time for an answer.

'Shall I start telling jokes?' Ross asked.

'Oh, Mamma's just an original philosopher,' Kelly explained. 'She's a one-woman dating service, immigration bureau and travel agency, and she can't stand to see anyone who isn't smiling.'

He raised a dark eyebrow. 'I can see the dating service,' he said, winding spaghetti around his fork, 'but what about the rest?'

'She promises jobs to Italians who want to immigrate or come here to school. They work here for a year, and then they go on to other jobs and she brings over someone else. There are an amazing number of Italian kids at the University—all of whom started out by waiting at tables for Mamma.'

'And the travel agency?'

'Didn't you know that everyone should visit Italy?'

'I see. Well, she can certainly make spaghetti.'

'The mushrooms are fresh, you know.' She toyed with one, pushing it around with her fork, and decided to try a different approach. 'What do you do, Ross? I don't know anything about you.'

'I travel for a chain of department stores.'

'On the West Coast?'

'All over the country, actually. But I'm based in Chicago.'

'Which store?'

He seemed reluctant to tell her anything at all. 'Tyler-Royale,' he said finally.

'Oh.' It was one of the largest chains in the nation. Kelly had never been in a Tyler-Royale store, but everyone had heard the name. 'Are you a buyer, or something?'

'Not really.' But he made no effort to explain.

Travelling salesman, she thought. And he doesn't want to admit that he's one of the less-important fish. 'Why did Patrick name you in his will, and not your mother?' she asked.

'Damned if I know,' Ross muttered.

He really did have a nice face, she reflected. It was strong and square, and with that gorgeous winter tan— whatever he'd been doing on the West Coast, it hadn't all been inside a department store!

His smile flashed. 'Maybe he knew she already owned a set of bone china,' he said. 'Look, what makes you think you can run a bookstore, anyway? Do you have any experience in retail sales?'

'Well, I worked in a dress shop one summer,' she admitted reluctantly. 'But my degree——'

'A college education provides wonderful initials after your name,' he said, 'but it usually doesn't make much difference when it comes to holding down a job.'

'Or even getting one,' she said bitterly. 'I was laid off months ago from the only real job I ever had, and now I can't get any kind of work. I'm overqualified—

everyone is hiring the kids who are still in school
because they work cheaper.'

'So why stay here? There are other towns.'

'Because I like it here.' And because other towns
don't have Allen, she added to herself. Before she had
met Allen, she had thought about moving away. She
had always intended to go home, after she got her
degree. But then both of her parents had died in the
space of a few months, and there was no home to go
back to. So she had stayed. Now, of course, this would
always be her home—hers and Allen's.

Ross grunted assent, and broke a piece of hot bread
from the loaf.

'As for being experienced, I worked in the other
bookstore for a while.'

'I was thinking that there must be an official
bookstore somewhere around here. Patrick certainly
didn't supply all the textbooks for the university.'

'It isn't official. I mean, it isn't part of the college or
anything, but Olsen—the owner—has the gall to call it
the University Bookstore.'

'How long did you work there?'

'A day and a half,' she admitted reluctantly.

'A day——' He looked up in astonishment. 'Why did
you quit? Didn't like the work?'

'Sure, I liked it. I just didn't like the boss, and he
liked me too well.'

'What does that mean?'

'Use your imagination, Ross.'

'Made a pass at you, did he?'

'For the whole day and a half. I'd like to show that
slimy animal a thing or two.'

'The lady wants her revenge.'

'That's part of it,' she admitted.

'What makes you think you can compete with him?'

'Simple. Olsen makes a killing on used textbooks—he
buys them from the students for a dollar or two and
then sells to the next student for ten. I can pay more,

sell for less, and take over that business. I'm amazed Patrick never did that. Do you know, I never even knew Patrick's store was there——'

He was shaking his head. 'You're a lamb in the wilderness, Kelly.'

'What does that mean?'

'As soon as you cut your profit margin, the other store will follow. Even if they end up losing money, they won't let you take that market away from them.'

His voice was gentle. She looked up uncertainly. 'They won't? she asked.

'No, my dear. They won't. And you can't afford to lose money. They can—at least for long enough to drive you out of business.'

'But that's not fair——'

'I'm afraid that fairness doesn't enter into it.' He sounded abstracted, almost absent-minded. 'I'm amazed that you didn't see some advantage in co-operating with the man, Kelly.'

She was furious, too angry to care about whether she was throwing away her last chance of persuading him. 'For your information, I am not interested in sleeping my way into a job. And regardless of what you think, I did not befriend your uncle just so I could be written into his will. If I'd wanted to do that, I'd have made sure you were written out! So just shut up, Mr Ross Clayton!' She dashed tears from her eyes.

'There, there. Perhaps that was a little strong,' he conceded.

'You're damned right it was!'

'Mr Clayton?' At the sound of the honey-smooth voice, they both looked up in surprise. Ross rose, a question in his eyes.

'Hello, Mr Olsen,' Kelly said, with careful emphasis on the name.

Ross raised an eyebrow.

'I understand you're in town to settle Patrick's affairs,' said the owner of the University Bookstore. 'I couldn't help overhearing your name, and I thought perhaps we could make a deal that would benefit both of us.'

'I'm listening,' Ross said. Kelly started to protest, and he made a gesture that shut her off in the middle of a word.

'I buy a lot of books, you know,' Mr Olsen said. He ran a hand back over his oiled black hair. 'I'd like to make an offer on Patrick's stock. I'm not interested in the lease or anything, just the books. Shall we say, five hundred dollars?'

'Five hun——' Kelly started to say.

Ross cut across her protest ruthlessly. 'I'll think about it, Mr—Olsen, was it?'

'That's right,' the man smiled. 'Here's my card. I'll be expecting you to drop in and chat with me.'

As soon as he had turned away, Kelly snapped, 'But Mr Bradford said——'

'Would you shut up?' Ross hissed, and Kelly obediently closed her mouth.

He waited until the door had closed behind Mr Olsen. 'If you're going to go into retail sales, my girl, the first thing you need to learn is when to keep your mouth shut.'

'But Mr Bradford said the stock was worth at least two thousand!'

'And if you'd said that, he would know just as much as you do.'

She bit her tongue. He was right.

'And if you're going to take that slimy animal on, the less he knows about your business, the better,' he added quietly.

It took a moment to sink in. Then she said, her voice shaking, 'You're going to let me do it?'

'Six months,' he warned. 'You said you could do it in six months. If it isn't showing a profit, however small, in that time, then——' He made a chopping motion with one hand. 'I'll file a partition action, or whatever it takes.'

'You won't have to,' she said. 'If I fail, then I'll agree to sell. But I can do it,' she said. There was a glow in her eyes. 'I know I can!'

'We'll see,' he said. 'We'll see. It isn't going to be a picnic, you know.'

CHAPTER THREE

SHE was at the bookstore early the next morning, determined to show Ross that she wasn't just playing a game, that she was willing to work hard to get the store back on its feet. She tied a scarf over her hair, rolled up the sleeves of her flannel shirt, and looked around, wondering where on earth she should begin.

'The only sensible place to start is the coffeepot,' she told herself finally, and scrubbed out the big urn that stood on a table beside the fireplace. A smaller, more efficient percolator would have to be one of the first things she moved over from her own apartment, she thought as the aroma began to sift through the store.

She threw the casements in the bay windows open. Better cold, fresh air than none at all, she decided.

Half an hour later, Joe Keswick's creaky voice said from the stairs, 'Do I smell coffee?'

'Sure. Come on down and help yourself.'

He did, with a grin. 'Couldn't rightly tell,' he admitted, 'if I was smelling the coffee or your cleaning soap. Come to think of it, Patrick's coffee always kind of tasted like the soap.' He settled himself into a rocking chair. 'Looks like you won the fight with your young man,' he observed.

'What do you mean?' Kelly asked absently. She was methodically taking piles of books off the shelves, dusting the shelf, and then returning as many volumes as would fit comfortably. The rest she was stacking on the floor. If I don't run out of floor first, she thought, I should have all the shelves dusted this morning.

'You seem to be getting ready to open the place again,' Joe Keswick said.

'Oh. Yes, but I wouldn't call that winning the fight. And he isn't my young man. We're partners.'

'Oh?' Joe looked around vaguely. 'Then where is he?'

'Excellent question.' Kelly had been wondering about that herself. She didn't even know where he was staying. After the astonishing about-face he'd made last night, she'd been afraid to press for any further information. He had taken her back to Mr Bradford's office, followed her home to be sure she got there safely on her bike and waved goodbye—— So much for being my young man, she thought. Joe Keswick and Mamma would both be upset if they knew she hadn't got even a handshake, much less a good night kiss!

And that's enough of that silliness, she told herself. If he'd tried anything of the sort, I would have called the cops.

There was a plaintive meow from the bay window, and Kelly jumped.

'It's just Rapunzel back home,' Joe told her. 'She comes and goes as she wants. That's why Patrick installed the cat door in that window pane.'

'Terrific. That's all I need—a cat-about-town.' Then she said, 'Or do you want to keep Rapunzel?'

Joe shuddered. 'What would I want with that cat? I've put up with her for months, since Patrick first got sick. No, the cat's yours.'

'In that case, we'd better start by making friends.' Kelly climbed down off the ladder and cautiously approached the bay window. Rapunzel was seated, like the queen she was, atop a stack of books, staring impassively at Kelly. She was a calico, with pure white paws and face, and patches of black, brown and orange on her head and down her back. 'Aren't you gorgeous?' Kelly breathed. She held out a hand. Rapunzel sniffed it gingerly and let out a piteous meow.

'You miss Patrick, don't you?' Kelly murmured. She stroked the cat's chin, and Rapunzel managed to look indecently pleased at having found a human who understood the proper way to pay respect to a cat. Kelly noted the cat's rounded stomach and said,

'Obviously she's been out before. I see we have another generation on the way.'

'Always do,' Joe said genially.

'What did Patrick do with all of the kittens?'

'Oh, there was usually people waiting for 'em. Can't say I understand why.' He looked at the animal with a jaundiced eye.

The front door opened, and Ross came in. 'Taking a break?' he asked politely, seeing Kelly with the cat. 'Or were you waiting for me?'

Kelly's temper flared. 'I've been up on a ladder for an hour. Where have you been?'

'Having a charming and very informative chat with Mr Olsen at the University Bookstore.'

Kelly was stunned. He had gone behind her back and talked to that skunk? If he'd made some sort of deal—— 'Why, you—you traitor!' she snapped.

Rapunzel, incensed that Kelly had stopped petting her, leaped down from the bay window and settled herself in the spare rocking chair for a bath and a snooze.

Ross pulled a notebook out of his pocket. 'He raised his offer to a thousand, and——'

'I suppose you think we ought to take it!'

He really did have a beautiful smile, she had to admit. It lit up his eyes with a mischievous sparkle. Maybe he wasn't quite as tense all the time as she had thought. 'Of course not,' he said. 'I just thought you'd like to know that the stakes are going up.'

Kelly tried to get her breath back. She didn't have the least idea if she should trust him. 'Then if you weren't making a deal, why were you talking to him at all?'

'I was buying a little time,' he said. 'I didn't tell him about you, of course. I did say that I'd think about his undoubtedly generous offer, but that I couldn't promise any decision until I'd had a chance to look through the books. Olsen won't do anything drastic for the next week or so, as long as he thinks I might accept his offer. So we can get the jump on him.'

'Oh,' Kelly said softly.

'Now, admit it, Kelly. I'm not such a bad guy to have around, am I?'

She shook her head. 'After last night, though, I expected you to be more of a silent partner.'

That charming smile flashed again. 'Me? Silent?' he asked.

'I guess that was asking a little too much,' Kelly admitted.

'Besides, he might keep increasing his offer. And who knows, we might actually decide to sell.'

'Never!' She climbed her ladder again. 'Though some of this stuff is pretty old,' she called down. 'I found a recipe book a few minutes ago that calls for ten cents' worth of ground beef to make meat loaf.'

'Hang on to it. That may be all you can afford by the time this experiment is over,' he recommended. 'Are you positive you don't want to take his offer? I'm not sure this whole store is worth a thousand dollars.'

'I'm sure,' she said briefly.

Ross shrugged. He took his jacket off and tossed it across the counter. 'Well, you'll have to get rid of a lot of it to make room for new books. You'll need a gimmick when you first open, to draw people in and get rid of a lot of this stuff.'

'I don't think Patrick ever advertised, did he?'

'You're going to have to,' Ross warned. He started to carry the stacks of books she was discarding to tables in the front of the store.

'Oh, I know. I've been thinking about it. What if I sold used books by the pound? People buy carrots and cabbage and sugar by weight all the time, but selling books that way should get some attention.'

There was a long silence, so long that she thought for a moment that he was trying to find a polite way to tell her she was an idiot. Finally, he said thoughtfully, 'It's crazy enough it just might work—and heaven knows we have enough of a supply!' He picked up another heavy stack.

She was so startled at the note of respect in his voice that she almost fell off her ladder.

Joe Keswick, who had dozed off in his chair, woke with a start. 'Time for my walk,' he announced, stretching. 'Nice to see you young people working together like this.'

He shuffled off down the sidewalk, and Ross stood thoughtfully looking after him for a long moment. 'I'd forgotten he was still here,' he said finally.

'Yes,' Kelly teased. 'The first thing to learn about retail sales is when not to talk.'

Ross didn't share the joke. 'And I just violated the rule,' he agreed.

'He's the landlord, for heaven's sake. He isn't going to tell anyone our secrets.'

'I'd be more comfortable if he didn't know any more of them. Are you finding anything up-to-date?'

Kelly put her head around the corner of a set of shelves. 'Let's put it this way,' she said. 'You know about the great revolution in technology since the invention of the computer? The closest we come to high-tech literature is a book on the fundamentals of the slide rule.'

'I thought they'd stopped using those.'

'They have.'

'I see.' There was a long silence, and then Ross said, 'Here's the complete works of Charles Dickens, for heaven's sake.'

'What's so bad abut that? At least it's a recognisable name.'

'The original printing?'

'Let me see that!' Kelly came down the ladder in two steps. 'You're joking!'

'Unfortunately, yes. It is the complete works, however—fancy leather binding and all.'

'Don't do that to me again,' Kelly begged. 'My heart can't take it. Do you know what a first edition Charles Dickens would be worth?'

He looked thoughtful, and then hazarded a guess. 'Lots?'

'That's a safe guess. Besides, I don't think there was actually any such thing. His work was printed in newspapers and in pamphlet form first, not in books.'

'How do you know all this stuff?'

'I went to college, remember?'

'I did, too, but I didn't hear all this.'

'What did you graduate in? Surfing?' she asked sweetly.

Ross gave her a patient smile. They worked in silence for several minutes, Kelly taking books down, Ross arranging them in neat rows on the tables.

'Do you have your work scheduled for this afternoon?' he asked a little while later.

'I thought I'd start to clean upstairs. If I can get the mess reduced up there and move in by the end of the week, I won't have to pay another month's rent where I'm living.'

'Are you still determined to move here?'

'Why on earth shouldn't I? We're paying for the apartment; I might as well use it.'

'The inconvenience of living right upstairs from your business, for one. You'll be able to hear the phone every time it rings.'

'And on the other hand,' Kelly retorted, coming down the ladder with another stack of discards, 'there is the convenience of not having to ride my bike in the snow, rain, sleet or heat to get to work. Or the sheer luxury of having a place of my own after having split costs with three other girls for what seems forever. If I have to take my choice——'

He was silent for a long moment, chewing his bottom lip.

Finally she said, 'Why should you object to me living here? It'll save you money, too. Business inconvenience wasn't the reason, was it?'

He shook his head, and said, 'You can't live here with that dirty old man in the next apartment.'

What dirty—— Do you mean Joe Keswick? He's a sweetheart!'

'Yeah, especially when he's waving a shotgun around. He's really charming then.'

'It wasn't loaded!'

'How do you know? The man could go off his nut any minute——'

Kelly rewarded him with a smile. 'How sweet of you to be concerned about me,' she said, and patted him on the head. He really could be a nice guy, she realized, and wondered if there was a woman waiting for him somewhere who knew that too. Didn't travelling salesmen have a girl in every town?

'I'm just looking out for myself,' he said. 'If you get murdered in your bed, I'll be the prime suspect.'

'And then you'd have all of this to go through again,' she added cheerfully. 'Nevertheless, I plan to move in upstairs, just as soon as I can get the clutter isolated so there's a place to sleep.'

'I don't suppose there's any way to change your mind? No, I thought not. I think we need to spend the afternoon with Mr Bradford, getting the legal stuff straightened out, and then stop at the bank to apply for a loan.'

She stopped halfway back up the ladder. 'A loan? Why?'

'Because you're going to need capital to get started. You'll have to spend a bundle before you can even open the door.'

'But—a bank loan. I don't know——'

'Where else did you propose to get the money for new stock, for advertising, for——?'

'Mr Bradford said there was a little money in a savings account.'

'Darned little.' He sighed. 'Look, Kelly, you have to have a credit rating before suppliers will let you have books on consignment. And you don't have one.'

She bit her lip. 'All right,' she said finally.

'Trust me,' he said. 'It's the only way.'

'But I don't. Trust you, that is. You want me to fail!'

'Believe it or not, my dear, I don't.'

'Well, I'm paying it back just as soon as I can,' she called from the top of the ladder.

'That's the idea.'

'Just how long are you planning to stick around and manage my business?' she asked tartly.

'Don't you mean—our business?' he reminded gently. 'I'll be here a week or so—long enough to get Patrick's personal property settled, and help you out with a few pointers.'

Kelly said sweetly, from the top of the ladder, 'Be sure to give me plenty of notice, and I'll throw the biggest bon-voyage party you've ever seen. By the way, if you stumble across a book on raising cats, save it for me.'

'Rapunzel?' he asked, with foreboding.

'It's just a guess—but I'd say in another couple of weeks I'll have a litter of new mascots.'

'Just what I always needed,' Ross grumbled.

'Think positive,' she recommended. 'You won't be here.'

'Perhaps not—but something tells me I'll never quite get over this experience. First he saddled me with you, then the cat,' he complained. 'What did I ever do to Patrick to make him treat me like this?'

'You're going to do what?' Allen sounded horrified. He paced across the crowded living-room of her apartment, and came back to his place on the couch.

'Do you really want me to go through it all again?' Kelly's voice was sharp. Allen was being difficult, and she was tired of explaining herself to everyone.

'No. Hearing it once was bad enough. I knew when you weren't home last night that something strange was going on, but this beats everything.'

'I'm sorry I didn't call you when I got in, but it was late, and——'

'Yes, I heard that you and what's-his-name were
enjoying yourself at Mamma Mia's.'

'We were having a serious discussion over dinner,'
she corrected. 'And who told you that?'

He didn't look convinced, and he didn't answer. 'So
you're going to start a new business? Kelly, you don't
know anything about running a store——'

'It's not exactly a new business,' she parried.
'Actually, I'm reopening an old one.'

'With a partner that you know nothing about.'

That was true, and she was uneasily aware of it. What
did she know about Ross Clayton, after all? The fact that
he was Patrick's nephew meant less than nothing; for all
she knew, Patrick might not have seen him in years. The
man might be anything from a safecracker downwards,
and Patrick wouldn't have known.

But there was no point in telling Allen any of that.
He was already upset enough. She said, carefully, 'Ross
travels for the Tyler-Royale department stores.'

'Doing what?'

'He didn't exactly say.'

'That figures. He could be an organised shop-lifter
and still meet that definition, Kelly. He could be a con
man——'

She was tired of fighting about it. She was not only
physically exhausted from the hard work, but she was
still in shock over the size of the loan that Ross had
thought it necessary to get from the bank. Even the fact
that the loan officer had insisted that Ross also sign the
papers wasn't making her feel any better.

She hadn't told Allen about the loan. She decided
that what he didn't know, he couldn't yell at her
about. But what if he was right, and Ross was some sort
of con artist? She'd be left holding the bag.

Well, it wouldn't be for long, she thought. In another
week, Ross Clayton would be on his way back to
Chicago, and she'd be starting out a new era in her life,
with six months to prove herself.

You can do it, Kelly, she told herself stoutly.

'Look, Allen,' she pleaded, 'I'm committed to this thing——'

'Crazy,' he said, shaking his head. 'Very crazy.'

'So what am I supposed to do? I can't just sit around for ever, waiting for a job to drop into my lap. I have to do something to make a life for myself, and a bookstore is the ideal opportunity.'

'Complete with mysterious partner,' he grumbled. 'If you'd only asked me for my advice——'

'Sorry,' she snapped. 'I realise, of course, that after almost a year of law school you know much more than Mr Bradford does, but——'

'Ouch.' Allen had the grace to grin. 'All right, Kelly, you win. The bookstore it is, and I hope you don't fall on your face.'

One of her room-mates sidled through the living-room just then, wearing a nightgown and a facial mask, and Allen grimaced. 'It will have one advantage,' he admitted, 'at least you'll have your own apartment. The way it is, with Mother having a fit about you being unladylike every time you call me at the house, and the four-ring circus here, we never get a moment alone.'

She smiled at him, and her face lit up. 'Kissing shouldn't be a spectator sport,' she agreed.

'That's my girl,' he said, and put an arm around her. Kelly relaxed against him with a sigh.

Then another room-mate yelled, 'Dammit, Kelly, I just tripped over those boxes you left in the hall. When are you going to move that junk?'

'Tomorrow!' Kelly called back. 'And not a minute too soon for me,' she murmured into Allen's ear. 'We can finally find out what it's like to be alone.'

It sounded wonderful. To be able to invite him over without checking with anyone else, to use the kitchen without first having to clean up the mess someone else had made, to have a bathroom with only her own things in it——

'In the meantime,' Allen said reluctantly, 'I've got a test tomorrow, and I'd better hit the books.' He kissed her again, lightly, and left.

She curled up on the couch, her chin in her hand, and sat there for a long time. Her lips curved into a secret smile as she thought about Allen. He was a dear, really he was. And if the bookstore worked out——

If she could turn a profit in the first six months, she thought, then maybe they wouldn't have to wait till he was finished at law school after all. As it was, his parents were paying his tuition fees, and he was living at home to help keep the costs down. But if they had a place to live, then——

She lost herself in pleasant dreams for a while, thinking how wonderful it would be if they didn't have to wait two more years. To be his wife—to have a real part in earning that law degree that would mean security for both of them in future years—that was what love really was.

If only the bookstore worked out, she thought, and wondered if Ross was going to let her have an honest try at it, or if he was merely playing a game of cat and mouse—with Kelly being the mouse. Was he setting her up to fail, making it impossible for the store to succeed? After all, she had agreed that if it wasn't profitable in six months that she would sell her share without a fight. What if he had decided that fighting her now would be a waste of time, that he could wait a few months and accomplish his goal without a struggle?

The size of that loan still scared her. It didn't seem necessary to have that kind of money to draw on, just to get a little store started again. Fright fluttered deep in the pit of her stomach. She couldn't hope to sell enough books in six months to pay back that loan.

Or what if he walked off with the cash? What if it was all an elabarate con to get thousands of dollars of cash and then disappear, leaving her to pay it back?

She pictured his face, in her mind. Those dark blue

eyes, so serious and straightforward, and yet with a twinkle always lurking underneath, it seemed—they were honest eyes. And his face, tanned and strong, with a firm chin and a nose that had character—it was an honest face.

'And if anything, that ought to scare you more,' she told herself crossly, under her breath. 'A con man who didn't look honest wouldn't make much of a living at his profession, that's for sure.'

When the telephone rang she stretched out a hand to answer it without a thought. Ross said, 'You must have been sitting on top of the phone, waiting for the boyfriend to call.'

'Not at all, because he just left. What do you want?'

'So early?' He sounded genuinely concerned. 'Did you have a fight about you moving into that lonely apartment?'

'As a matter of fact, Ross, he approves,' she said sweetly.

'Oh, I see.' From the tone of his voice, she thought he saw entirely too much. 'He's planning to move in with you, I take it?'

'Of course not. Why did you call, anyway? To rearrange my love life?'

He sounded horrified that she had any such suspicion. 'Kelly, I'm shocked. I would never interfere in anything so personal—so long as it didn't affect the business. Now if you take to spending more time in your apartment with him—what's his name?'

'I can't think why you'd need to know.'

'Because I'd hate to have to refer to him as the boyfriend all the time. It's belittling, actually, for a full-grown man to be called that.'

He sounded perfectly sincere, but Kelly didn't believe a word of it.

When the silence had dragged on for a full minute, Ross sighed. 'I see that I'll have to wait for an introduction. I've been thinking about it all evening,

Kelly. I think we may have to readjust our thinking on the bookstore.'

Her hand clenched on the receiver. 'If you think that you can talk me into selling out now——' she said, fury building in her voice.

'Do you always lose your temper before you listen to the whole story?' he asked plaintively.

'Only when I know I'm not going to like what I hear.'

'Well, it must save you a lot of time. Honestly, you can get mad faster than any other woman I've ever met.'

'I suppose you've run a survey of thousands!'

'Well, at least hundreds,' he said genially. 'If you'll remember, the loan officer at the bank wasn't impressed with your small experience at managing a business——'

'So what? How does anyone get experience, anyway?'

'And since I had to sign my name to the loan as well, I must admit that I'm not terribly enthusiastic about turning that sort of money over to you, either.'

'Good. I never wanted the loan in the first place.'

He ignored the interruption and went smoothly on. 'At any rate, I called my boss this afternoon, and asked for a leave of absence.'

'A leave——' She felt as if she'd just been hit in the stomach with a baseball bat. 'You're staying here?'

'At least for a couple of months. Enough to get you started——'

'Or sabotage me!'

He sounded hurt. 'Kelly, Kelly. Why would I do that? I'd be throwing my money away as well as yours. I want the store to succeed—otherwise I'll be paying that loan back for the rest of my life.'

'It's my loan,' she said stiffly.

'You might see it that way,' he agreed, 'and I might see it that way, but the bank has definitely different ideas. At any rate, I'll be staying as long as you need me—the full six months if necessary.'

Kelly said tartly, 'It can't have been much of a job, if they aren't going to miss you for six months.'

'They owe me a vacation. And my boss assured me that if I was needed, she'd call.' His voice was airy. 'I can be in Chicago in a few hours, straighten them out, and pop right back here——'

'You work for a woman?'

'Why not?' He sounded puzzled. 'The only other choice I had was working for a man.'

'That explains it. I'll bet you have her in the palm of your hand.'

'Lovely woman. You'd like her.'

'I'll just bet I would!' She thought that he sounded like a cat who had just finished off a pitcher of cream. 'Ross, what if I don't want your——' She thought about it, and decided to be diplomatic'—your help?'

'Sorry, darling, you can't get rid of a partner. Mr Bradford's already told you that. I've got some wonderful ideas, by the way. I called a friend in the book department of the anchor store——'

'Another woman, no doubt,' she said drily.

'No. Oliver has some wonderful ideas. But all that can wait till tomorrow. I'll see you at the store, bright and early!'

Before she could protest, the phone line was dead. She sat there with it in her hand for a long time.

CHAPTER FOUR

KELLY was bone-weary. She curled up on the windowseat in her new apartment and looked down to the street, where lights from the bay windows in the front of the bookstore still fell across the pavement. Thank heaven it was Ross's turn to work the evening shift, she thought. She didn't think she could stand to smile at one more customer today.

The Bookworm had been open for almost a week, and the pace hadn't let up. She had to admit that Ross—or, more likely, his friend in the book department at Tyler-Royale—had been right about a lot of things. Advertising, for one, and the need for an extra pair of hands. Ross had taken over the ad-campaign and smiled his way to a better rate than Kelly had thought possible. Of course, she thought, give the devil his due, the saleswoman had been impressed with those bedroom blue eyes. But he had been a welcome extra pair of hands——

She looked down at her own. Her fingers were almost trembling with weariness. Much as she hated to admit it, Ross had indeed been a good man to have around. She couldn't possibly have done it alone. They had decided to keep the store open the maximum number of hours this first week, to take full advantage of the advertising. At no time had the store really been crowded, but there had been a respectable number of patrons all the time, and all the climbing up and down the ladders to find what the customers wanted had worn her out. She'd be glad when they got on to a normal schedule next week.

Allen handed her a bowl of buttered popcorn and leaned over to steal a kiss.

'I'm just too tired,' she protested.

He looked irritated, but he said merely, 'It'll slow down next week.'

'I hope so. And yet, it was well worth it. I'll bet we've got rid of half of those old books downstairs.'

Allen shook his head. 'You still have the ones up here. You'd have been better off selling them all to the guy at the other bookstore. Let him find a place to store them.' He looked with disfavour at the row of boxes that still lined one wall of Kelly's apartment. 'You'll be years getting rid of them all.'

'Don't remind me. They're all over the place.' There had been no time to sort the books that had filled the apartment; she had no time to spare in moving. So she had, in self-defence, simply picked up every volume in the room and put them into boxes.

'I still think you should have sold them.'

'Ross thought we needed a loss-leader to get customers to come in. He says that selling them by the pound was an ingenious idea——'

'Ross says. Ross says. Do you know how many times you've told me that in the last week?' Allen snapped.

She was startled at his vehemence. 'I'm sorry, Allen, but I can't help it if the bookstore is all I have on my mind. After all, from the time I get up in the morning till I go to bed at night, all I see is books.'

'And Ross,' Allen said, under his breath.

Kelly gestured towards the boxes. 'It's a wonder I don't dream about books. And if you think it's bad in here, go look in Ross's living room. He hasn't even picked his up yet—they're still all over the floor.'

'And why he had to move in here is more than I understand,' Allen grumbled.

'Honestly, Allen. Where else was he supposed to live?'

Rapunzel pushed open the connecting door between the two apartments and crossed the room, her walk a little less graceful now that the time for her kittens to be born was drawing near.

Allen looked at the open door with irritation in his eyes. 'You work with the guy all day, and you're practically living with him,' he said. 'Why don't you at least lock that damned door? If he wants something, he can knock. You don't know what he'll do——'

'The cat is very unhappy with the door closed,' Kelly said. She put her empty popcorn bowl down on the floor and leaned back against the pillows, drawing her feet up under her. 'She's always on the wrong side of it, you see. And you haven't heard anything till you've listened to a very aggravated, very pregnant cat voice her disapproval.'

'I still think that it would be only smart to lock the door——'

She sat up again and forced a smile. 'Believe me, I'm in no danger from Ross,' she said. 'He's every bit as tired as I am these days. Besides, there's a woman in Chicago who would skin him alive if she caught him with another girl.'

'Oh?'

'Yeah. She shipped some clothes out here for him, and on top of the first box was a colour photo. It's one of those misty, seductive things, and she's wearing a négligé.'

'Half naked?'

'Oh, no. Actually, it might be an evening gown—but it certainly looks like a négligé.'

'I'd have expected a nude.'

'Why?'

Allen shrugged. 'He just seems the sort.'

'Well, she couldn't be any more unforgettable, no matter what she was or wasn't wearing. And she obviously doesn't intend to be forgotten, or she wouldn't have sent him the picture. Frankly, I wouldn't be surprised if she turns up on the doorstep some day.'

'Well, Ross Clayton's love life is no concern of mine. Or yours either, come to that,' he warned.

'The thing that puzzles me,' Kelly said thoughtfully,

'is that he opened the box, picked up the picture, laughed, and set it on top of the refrigerator—as if it didn't have any effect on him at all.' She didn't see the growing irritation on Allen's face. 'But now,' she continued, 'it's on the coffee table in there—as if he looks at it a lot.'

'It's probably his wife,' he growled. 'Now can we let your partner and his mysterious lady rest in peace and enjoy ourselves?

She looked at him in sudden surprise. 'Oh,' she said finally. 'I did it again, didn't I?'

He nodded. 'Come here and give me a kiss and let's forget about him.'

It was a nice kiss. It was so pleasant, Kelly thought dreamily, not to have to be continually alert for a room-mate walking through. And having Allen all to herself—that was heaven. She sighed, and relaxed in his arms, thinking about the days to come when they would be married and they could be together every night . . .

A harsh buzz startled her, and she pulled away from Allen.

'What the devil——?' he asked.

'It's the panic button in the shop. I was scared to work alone at night, so Ross put in the buzzer so if I needed help I could ring for him.'

Allen's eyes surveyed her tiny, trim figure. 'So why is he calling for *you*?' he asked tartly. 'I hardly think the thieves will run when they see you coming.'

'He probably just doesn't know where to find something, because I stocked most of the shelves. I'll be right back.'

'Yeah. Sure,' Allen muttered. 'The guy has rotten timing. I might as well make some more popcorn.'

Kelly turned at the door and smiled at him. 'It does taste awfully good,' she agreed. 'I never did have supper.'

There were only a couple of customers in the store, and as she came down the spiral staircase, Ross pointed towards one who was browsing through the new fiction. Kelly wondered why he couldn't handle the sale himself. She'd been handling four or five at once, all week.

Then she saw who the customer was. 'Hi, Cathy!' she said. 'What brings you out this late at night?'

Cathy grinned. 'I just had to see how you were doing. Besides, I need to order a special medical text, and Ross thought——'

So he was on a first-name basis with the customers already, Kelly thought. She looked up Cathy's book and jotted the order down.

'I didn't think Olsen needed the business,' Cathy said. 'We miss you at the hospital, badly. I don't think anyone realised how much difference one volunteer could make.'

'Well, that's flattering. I miss it too, of course. But I've been a little busy around here.' She waved a hand towards the bookshelves, the wood now gleaming under the soft lights. The freshly painted walls, the bright coloured chintz that covered new cushions on the rocking chairs—it had taken a tremendous amount of time, but the little shop was now an inviting place to come and browse.

'I must admit, I'm surprised,' Cathy said.

Kelly didn't pretend to misunderstand. 'It's funny, isn't it, how we all misread Patrick?' She looked around again, and said softly, 'O'Hara's legacy. I miss him an awful lot, Cathy.'

Cathy shivered. 'It must be like living with a ghost,' she said.

'In a way, it is. As we were cleaning, I kept running across notes Patrick had left for himself. But he's a pleasant ghost.'

'Nevertheless,' Cathy said, 'I wouldn't like it. Call me when my book comes in.'

'Of course.' Kelly waited till the door had closed behind her friend, and then turned to Ross, who was checking an order off against the packing invoice. 'You couldn't write down the name of a medical text?' she asked.

He shrugged. 'She did ask for you.'

'Well, your timing is less than ideal. I have a guest upstairs.'

Ross raised an eyebrow. 'Sorry, I wasn't aware that you were doing something that couldn't be safely interrupted.'

Kelly flared, 'I wasn't—as if it was any of your business!'

'Then what's all the screaming about?' he asked mildly and returned to the invoice.

She swallowed hard and told herself that there was no way to win an argument with him, so she ought to know better than to start one. Then she climbed the spiral stairs again, her spine straight, trying to show him by her dignified bearing that he made no difference in her life. He didn't seem to notice.

Allen had spread his law books out on the tiny coffee table and was absorbed in his homework. Kelly poured herself a glass of milk and sat down beside him, just wanting to share his presence. How lovely it would be, she thought, when they could finally be together!

'Allen,' she said finally, snuggling up against him, 'do you suppose we could make it work if we got married soon? Instead of waiting till you graduate, I mean.'

For a moment, he didn't seem to have heard. Then he raised reluctant eyes from the law book.

She gave him a blinding smile, and threw her arms around him.

'Not now, Kelly,' he groaned. 'I'm trying to study!'

Disappointment flickered through her. 'But a few minutes ago——'

'I wasn't trying to study cases then. And as for this notion of getting married, my parents would never go for it.'

'But we could live here, over the store, and I'll be

earning enough for our living expenses. We'd still need help with your tuition, of course, but——'

'That's just it. If they're paying the tuition, they have something to say about how I spend my time.'

Kelly was getting angry. 'But how can they be so sure I wouldn't be good for you? They've never even met me!' Though, she was forced to admit, if there was any comunication at all between the partners in that law firm, Allen's father must by now have heard all about the temper tantrum she'd thrown in Roger Bradford's office that day, and that would not exactly leave him with a good impression.

I should have known better, she thought, and then defended herself. After all, Ross had provoked her beyond bearing. But whether John Parrish would take the Ross factor into account was doubtful.

'I haven't wanted to upset them.' Allen looked unhappy. 'They think I'm too young to make choices that will affect my whole life——'

'Well, don't let me push you into anything!' She stormed across the room, and then turned at the door. 'They're quite willing for you to be studying law. If you're old enough to choose a career, what's the big deal about choosing a wife?'

He started to protest, but she was out the door. As she descended the spiral stairs into the bookstore, she was already regretting what she had said. It wasn't very ladylike, after all, to have practically forced the man into setting a wedding date!

On the other hand, she thought rebelliously, it wasn't very flattering to be Allen's fiancée, so unofficially that she wasn't even sure what his parents looked like. And it wasn't very comfortable, either. It wasn't a good way to start a lifetime relationship with two people who were so obviously important to him . . .

'What's chasing you?' Ross asked lightly. 'If I didn't know better, I'd think you were fleeing from the boyfriend.'

'Not at all,' Kelly said with dignity. 'I came down for the order book so I can do some work.'

He tossed it across the counter to her. 'Is that why you're so uneasy tonight? Is your beau doing his homework instead of adoring you?'

'He takes his education very seriously,' Kelly responded stiffly. 'After all, once he has that degree, we'll both be secure for life. I won't have to scrimp and save any more.'

'Oh?' Ross sounded mildly interested. 'Does that mean you won't want to play games with the bookstore for ever?'

'I didn't say that.'

'He's such a conscientious boy, isn't he? Doing homework on a date.' He made a sympathetic clucking sound. 'Of course, that explains why you're angry——'

'I am not angry!' She heard the fury in her voice, and saw him start to smile. 'And it's not a date,' she said, forcing herself to sound calm. 'He just stopped by to spend the evening because he wanted to be with me.'

'And do homework.'

'He's working for our future. I can certainly understand why that's most important just now. And if you can't comprehend it——'

'Of course I can. After all, I'm spending the evening working for your future, too.'

The words fell into a sudden silence. 'Oh,' Kelly said, very softly. 'I'd forgotten that.'

'I thought you had.'

Chastened, she leaned on the glass-topped counter and watched as he counted the cash in the register. She knew so very little about him, she thought. 'If you were still in Chicago, what would you be doing tonight?' she asked curiously.

His hands paused, and his eyes grew dreamy. 'I'd go to dinner someplace quiet, with a lot of atmosphere— one of the places that tourists never find out about. And then up to Rush Street to one of the nightclubs——'

'With a lady?'

He looked at her as if she'd lost her mind. 'Of course, with a lady. I can hardly dance by myself, can I?' The long fingers replaced currency in the drawer.

'The lady whose picture is upstairs?' Kelly's voice was steady.

'Quite possibly.' He didn't look at her as he totalled the column of figures. 'We had an excellent day, Kelly. Sales are running far ahead of what I projected.'

'Good.' But she wasn't to be sidetracked. 'Is she your wife?'

His smile started in his eyes, she noticed. It sparkled there dangerously for several moments before it reached his mouth, and then he said, 'Why did Patrick call you Kelly Green?'

She was startled. Roger Bradford must have told him that, she thought, and wondered why it should bother her. It wasn't as if it was confidential information, after all. 'I'm not sure—except that he said with my name, I should be Irish.'

'I don't think it was the name,' he mused. 'I think it's the temper—you sound slightly Kelly Green with envy to me . . . If I were married to that lovely creature in the photograph, my dear, would I be here alone?'

Kelly was furious. It was just like him to take any enquiry as a personal question, and find some ulterior motive in it! Green with envy, was she? As if she could be romantically interested in him, with Allen waiting for her upstairs!

'Probably,' she snapped. 'She's no doubt enjoying the peace and quiet of having you gone!

'No, I'm sure she's missing me dreadfully. At least, she tells me that every time she calls,' he mused. 'Any other personal questions you'd like to have answered, while we're on the subject?'

'I should have insisted on a résumé before I took you on as a partner!' she said, goaded into irritability.

Ross shook his head sadly. 'You didn't take me on,

honey. I was thrust upon you.'

'If you wouldn't mind,' Allen said icily from the foot of the spiral stairs, 'I object to having my fiancée referred to as "honey" by another man.'

Ross's eyebrows went up, but he didn't comment.

'I've been thinking about it,' Allen went on, 'and you're absolutely right, Kelly. I'll talk to my mother tonight and ask her to invite you to the house to meet the family.'

Sudden fear choked Kelly's throat. 'If you really think——'

'Of course I do. If I'm old enough to be pursuing a career then I'm old enough to know what I want in a wife, and it's time they understand that. You'll be hearing from her.' He kissed her firmly, coolly, and started for the door, the stack of law books under his arm.

Ross reached for the key. 'I've already locked up,' he said. 'Go on upstairs, Kelly—I'll let the young man out, and I'll be up to join you in a minute.'

Kelly could feel her face burning. He hadn't said a single word that was off-colour, and yet he had implied that they'd be in bed together in a few minutes. And Allen had heard it, too; that was apparent. His jaw tightened, and then he made an obvious effort to overlook the comment.

Kelly retreated up the spiral stairs and went straight to her bedroom. She didn't think she could face Ross Clayton at the moment without scratching his handsome face. Tomorrow would be plenty of time to tell him what she thought of him.

Her bedroom had been Patrick's study, and here, too, boxes of books were piled along the walls. There was scarcely room for her bed, and Kelly thought wearily, when she tumbled into it, that she had to find time to start sorting out the mess and taking the excess books down to be sold.

It wasn't that she resented being surrounded by Patrick's things; as a matter of fact, it helped to ease the pain of missing the old man, when she could reach out for something that had been his. But sometimes it just seemed that there was so much work to be done that there was no escape from it, even in sleep. At least if her bedroom was clear, perhaps she'd be able to ignore the rest of the mess.

'I'll tackle it this weekend,' she told herself wearily. The store would not be open on Sundays; they had promised themselves one day off a week.

Just what I need, she thought wryly, punching her pillow up into a more comfortable shape. To spend my day off sorting through books—talk about a busman's holiday!

But sleep didn't come. She was just too tired to relax, she thought. Between the work itself and the anxiety, she was developing a horrible case of the what-ifs. What if the store failed? What if Allen's parents went along with the idea of their marriage, and then she couldn't support the two of them after all? Just a couple of weeks ago she'd been telling herself that it made much more sense to wait, instead of rushing into marriage. What had happened to that girl, the practical one?

She was shivering with fear by then. There's no sense in this, she told herself roundly. To lie here and worry won't get you to sleep any faster, and it certainly won't make the store run more smoothly if you're staggering around half-asleep tomorrow.

Plus, she realised a little vaguely, she could hear what sounded like a jazz band playing in her living-room. What on earth was Ross up to now, she wondered. If she could hear his stereo from her bedroom, then Joe Keswick must be having fits in the back apartment. She'd just have to bang on the connecting door and tell him to turn it down.

She crossed the living-room, pulling her terry robe on, and stopped dead when Ross said, from the shadows, 'If you're looking for me——'

'What are you doing in my living-room?' she protested. 'It's after midnight!'

'Because you have the only comfortable chair in the whole place,' he countered. 'Have you ever tried to sit in those things in my apartment?'

'Is that why the stereo is blaring?'

'Of course. What's the point of having music playing if I can't hear it?' He rose, then, and came towards her, saying softly, 'Just what did you come for, Kelly Green? I'm honoured, of course, whenever a woman shows up at my apartment door in her nightgown, but——'

'I want you turn that blasted music down so I can sleep,' she snapped. 'And you needn't get any notions that it was any more than that. Now if you'd get out of my apartment——'

Silently, without protest, he retreated into the other apartment. Without saying a word, however, he managed to leave the impression that he was a child who had been unfairly disciplined, and Kelly found herself standing in the middle of her living-room feeling unbearably guilty.

The noise level dropped to a bare murmur. She stood in the connecting door and said, 'That's better.'

'My pleasure,' he said. He was sitting stiffly upright on a straight-backed chair. 'Now do you think you can sleep?'

Not when I'm feeling guilty, she thought. 'Oh, come on back in,' she said finally, crossly.

He rewarded her with an angelic smile and resumed his relaxed position, this time on the couch with his feet propped up on the arm. 'Am I keeping you up?' he asked politely.

She stood there for a long moment. 'I'm scared,' she said finally, and her voice trembled.

'Come tell Uncle Ross all about it,' he said, and in that instant his voice had just a tinge of the rich burr of Patrick's. It brought tears to her eyes.

He sat up, and patted the cushion beside him. There was comfort in having his arm around her, and she sobbed out her fears in broken sentences into his shoulder.

'If the bookstore fails,' he said finally, 'then it fails. Most new businesses do, you know.'

'But——'

'It's not the end of the world. There will be something else.'

'But the loan—and Allen——'

His voice grew firmer. 'It's my opinion,' he said, 'which you are free to ignore if you want to that Allen should be left to take care of himself for a while.'

She looked up at him over her tissue. 'What do you mean by that?'

He shrugged. 'His parents have supported him all his life, and now you're volunteering to take over, and he's awfully young.'

'That's no crime! I'm even younger.'

'That's my point. You shouldn't be looking out for anyone but yourself just now. And neither should he. Until a man has supported himself for a while, and learned that it doesn't come easily, he doesn't hold much promise as a husband.'

'What makes you an authority?' Kelly asked stubbornly.

'Not personal experience, that's sure,' he said. 'I don't know what sort of husband I'd make—and I'll probably never find out.'

'Then how do you know all these things?'

He was silent, reluctant. Finally, he said, 'I watched a woman I love suffer through hell at the hands of a man who never in his life thought of anyone but himself.'

His voice was harsh with remembered pain, and Kelly put her head down on his shoulder. 'The woman in the picture?' she asked softly.

He looked down at her. 'How did you know that?'

Kelly shrugged. 'The way you looked at her, I guess.'

'She was a beautiful girl, soft and gentle. But he turned her into a hard woman.' He seemed to stop and think about it.

'What happened? she asked.

'Eventually, he killed himself in a car. But that was after he'd left scars on her that will never heal——'

And you still love her, Kelly thought. Well, it wasn't as if the idea was any surprise. She thought of that lovely face in the photograph, the cloud of dark hair, the beautiful mouth. And this time she saw in her memory other things—the faint shadow of strain in the big eyes, the tension in the mouth, the transparency of skin that came with illness.

Yes, that woman was scarred. After that, it would be no wonder if she hesitated to marry again. That haunted look in her eyes might explain why Ross had said he would never marry, Kelly thought. Was that why he was here? Did he hope that after a couple of months she would grow to miss him, and change her mind——

Her thoughts were beginning to circle wearily, but there was one thing she knew: he still loved her— whoever she was.

'Well,' he said abruptly. 'Enough about Whitney. That's history. We've come a long way from your fears of the bookstore closing.'

Whitney. So that was her name. It fitted her, Kelly thought vaguely. An aristocratic name for a woman who breathed elegance from every pore . . .

'Maybe you needed to talk about her,' she said.

'Perhaps I did.' He looked down at her, and there was an expression in his eyes that she had never seen before. 'Thank you, my dear,' he whispered, and kissed her softly.

She relaxed against him, the warmth of his body soothing her anxieties away. Nothing could hurt her while she was here, she thought a little vaguely. He would protect her.

How awful for him, she mused, that the woman he loved didn't feel the same way—confident of his protection, assured of his kindness. What misery it would be to love, and not have that love returned! I'm so lucky, she thought, to have Allen . . .

She wanted to hold Ross close, and soothe his pain, and assure him that Whitney would be better some day, that it would be all right.

There was a laugh in his voice as he said, 'Careful, Kelly. You might give a man the wrong ideas, acting like that.'

Abruptly, she realised that she had started to act on her thought. She didn't remember moving at all, but now his head was pillowed comfortably on her breast, and her cheek was pressed against his hair——

She uttered an embarrassed little screech and pulled away.

'And if Allen were to walk in——' Ross went on.

Kelly gathered the shreds of her dignity. 'A gentleman would forget that this ever happened,' she pointed out. 'He certainly would never speak of it.'

Now the laugh was real. 'But then, my dear, you've never given me credit for being a gentleman, have you?' he asked. He stretched lazily and added, 'I'd hate to disturb your opinion of me now. Off to bed, Kelly Green. Sweet dreams!'

CHAPTER FIVE

Joe Keswick was already in the bookstore when Kelly came down the next morning. He had lit the gas log in the fireplace and was rocking beside it, feet stretched out towards the flames, smoking a cigar.

'Waiting for your coffee, Joe?' she asked.

'Yup. And for the furnace to get back on the job. I've been down to work on it this morning.'

'I thought it was a little chilly in here.'

'It went on strike again.' He sounded resigned. 'We're gonna have a hot chequers game going here, as soon as the rest of the boys gather.'

'I ought to just give you the front door key,' she said mildly. Joe was almost always in the bookstore an hour before opening time, and she half-expected that one of these days she'd come down to find his friends waiting at the door, their noses pressed against the glass, impatient to get in . . .

At first it had bothered her, finding him there every morning. After all, even though he owned the building, he shouldn't have free run of the bookstore. But he was obviously doing no damage, so she had stilled her protests.

It was the morning coffee crowd that had really surprised her. The first day that the store was open again, there had been a steady influx of elderly men who had congregated around the fireplace, pulled up every chair in the place and a few boxes to seat the overflow, and spent the morning discussing the state of the world. They had been there every morning since, sometimes as many as a dozen of them, playing chequers, arguing politics, and drinking coffee. Mostly drinking coffee she thought. They never seemed to

agree on anything except the coffee, but they always
parted friends and came back for more. Today, because
it was Saturday, the crowd would be even bigger.

Joe had already filled the big coffee urn and plugged
it in. Kelly checked the supply of cream and sugar and
counted the change in the piggy bank that stood on the
tray beside the pot. Thirty-one cents, she noted. The
idea of an honour system to cover the cost of the
refreshments wasn't working out. 'Joe, you can tell the
boys that coffee costs a lot more than a penny a cup,'
she suggested. 'It's not that I want to make a profit on
it, exactly, but I have to break even.'

He looked disgruntled. 'Patrick never worried about
it,' he pointed out.

'I'm not Patrick. He was probably over here playing
chequers instead of running the store. But I'm trying to
make a living here, and I have a loan to pay off.'

'Okay, okay.' He put his head back against the chintz
cushion on the rocking chair and closed his eyes. 'I'll
take up a collection.'

'That's wonderful, Joe.' She found her own mug in
the stack beside the pot and filled it with lukewarm
coffee. It hadn't finished perking yet, but it would help
her get started.

'Put a nickel in the bank,' Joe ordered. He hadn't
even opened his eyes.

'That's the way,' she congratulated him. 'Assert
yourself, Joe.'

She took a long sip of the coffee, feeling the caffeine jolt
through her tired body. It had been a long time before she
had slept last night, for thinking about that embarrassing
few minutes when she had held Ross like a baby who
needed comfort. Foolish thought, she told herself. It had
probably all been a tall tale, told just to gain her
sympathy. A pretty girl whose life had been ruined, a
misunderstood man unbearably in love with her—it was a
story guaranteed to wring the heart of any woman. He
probably counted on that. There might not even be any

girl named Whitney, or she might mean nothing to him at all. The photograph was certainly no proof.

'But I bet a lot of women feel sorry for Ross when he gives them that line,' Kelly muttered. And you, my girl, almost fell for it too, she reminded herself.

She opened the box that she had carried downstairs that morning, and stacked the books from it on the counter. If she sorted out one boxful every day, she calculated, she could have her bedroom cleared out— 'In something like three months,' she groaned. It looked like a hopeless task.

But, she thought, if Patrick had cared enough about these books to take them up to his apartment, then there must have been something special about them. They were well worn, as if he had used them a great deal. She would have to judge the value of each volume separately, and there must be thousands of them still upstairs.

For one thing, she remembered abruptly, the family Bible hadn't turned up yet. She'd better keep a close eye out for that, because it belonged to Ross now, and not to the store. He had been unimpressed by the mention of the book when the will was read, but if it were sold accidentally he would probably have a fit. 'It must be somewhere up there,' she muttered.

And of course, she reminded herself, they hadn't yet unearthed the silver tea service that Patrick had left to her, either. Was it still up there somewhere, she wondered, or had the old man sold it and forgotten doing so?

It was probably at the back of a closet somewhere, she thought. She hoped that it would turn up. A silver tea service was about the least practical thing she could think of right now, but she could polish it up and dream of the future days when there would be a house to display it in. And it would be pleasant to have something that Patrick had cherished, that he had saved and cared for.

'Something besides books,' she muttered. She was beginning to feel as if she was drowning in books.

She unlocked the front door and from thin air, it seemed, two of Joe's morning companions appeared. 'We're sure glad to have a place to come again,' one of them said. 'Since Patrick died, this town hasn't been the same for us old-timers. 'Course, the coffee sure is better around here these days. Patrick's was awful.' He reached for his cup.

Kelly smiled. 'Watch out this morning. Joe made it.'

The other man winked at her. 'And not only the coffee is better,' he said in a conspiratorial whisper. 'The scenery sure has improved, too.'

'Charlie, you're a flirt,' Kelly told him, and started to the stock room with her empty box. The telephone interrupted her. 'We're getting an early start today,' she muttered under her breath.

It was a woman, asking for Ross. 'He hasn't come in yet this morning,' Kelly told her. 'May I help you?' Curiosity was like a forest fire inside her; the woman's voice was pleasant and low, with just a hint of a Virginia drawl. Was this Whitney? Somehow, she thought, it was the way she would expect her to speak ... Maybe there was a Whitney after all. And if she were calling Ross——

'You must be Kelly,' the woman speculated. 'I'm Maria Clayton. I would like to talk to Ross this morning, so would you tell him to be a good boy and call his mother?'

'Of course, Mrs Clayton.' Somehow she felt as if a weight had been removed from her shoulders. How foolish to go into a frenzy because some disembodied voice might belong to Whitney! That story of his couldn't be real, Kelly told herself irritably. She had asked him about the photograph, and he had seized the opportunity to spin her the yarn about poor Whitney.

'And tell him I'm shocked that he isn't at work yet.' But there was a teasing note in Mrs Clayton's voice.

'He worked late last night,' Kelly told her.

'That relieves my mind. I thought you might be spoiling him out there. I'd hate to have him forget that he has a perfectly good job waiting for him.'

Doing what? Kelly wanted to ask. Ross never had got round to telling her what his regular job was, or how long he planned to be away from it. It couldn't be too long, though, she thought. He couldn't keep up the payments on that sports car for long, with the small amounts of cash he was drawing from the bookstore. Be patient, Kelly lectured herself, and you'll have the store all to yourself soon.

'Tell me, how is the bookstore going?' Mrs Clayton asked.

'Much better than we expected for the first week. I have to give Ross the credit—he's obviously picked up a great deal of knowledge somewhere along the line.'

'Oh,' Mrs Clayton said cheerfully, 'as for that, department stores are a wonderful place to learn the retail business. I'm glad to know that he's absorbed something!'

'I'm not sure if it's him, or his friend in the book department,' Kelly added, incorrigibly honest.

Mrs Clayton laughed. 'I'm certain the Bookworm is no threat to Tyler-Royale,' she said. 'They should be glad to help you. By the way, Kelly, I wanted to thank you for all the care you gave Patrick when he was so ill.'

Was the comment a sarcastic one? It certainly didn't sound like it, but since all of Mrs Clayton's information came from Ross—— 'I enjoyed spending time with Patrick, Mrs Clayton.'

'And he liked to have you around, I'm sure. He didn't tell me he was ill, you know.

'He didn't?' So that was why there had been no visits, no flowers, no cards. And Ross must have thought that Kelly had kept Patrick from contacting his family.

'Patrick never wanted to be a bother to anyone.'

Maria Clayton sighed. 'At any rate, would you ask Ross to call me, Kelly?'

'Oh, here he comes now. It was nice to talk to you, Mrs Clayton.'

She handed Ross the phone and took the empty box back to the stockroom. She was about to toss it on to a pile when she heard a faint mew. 'Rapunzel,' she said aloud. 'All right, which box did you fall into this time?'

They tried to keep the cat out of the stockroom, because Rapunzel couldn't seem to learn that piles of empty boxes didn't make the best climbing towers. But she kept sneaking in, and usually she ended up trapped in a box, yelling to be rescued.

Kelly started through the boxes systematically, calling the cat's name in the hope that—with help on the way—Rapunzel would be smart enought to meow again. But there was only silence. 'Darn cat,' Kelly muttered. 'You'd think, as close as she is to having those kittens, that she'd be smart enough not to go bouncing around too much.'

In the far corner of the room, under a stack of boxes, two yellow eyes stared out at her. 'All right, how did you get back there?' Kelly asked as she started to clear a path. 'Well, come on, stupid cat.' But Rapunzel made no move to come out.

The reason was clear when Kelly finally reached the box. Two tiny furry creatures were snuggled at their mother's side, nursing greedily. One of them was a calico like Rapunzel, the other was almost pure black.

Kelly retreated quietly. Rapunzel's choice of location for her nursery was inconvenient enough; Kelly didn't want to frighten her into moving the kittens somewhere else.

Ross was looking through the stack of books when she came out. 'Did you know one of these lists the value of all the famous autographs?'

'No. How old is it?'

He checked. 'Old,' he said.

'But not old enough to be valuable, I'll bet. Put it on the sale table.'

'I used to have an autograph collection when I was a kid. Mind if I keep the book?'

'I certainly don't have any use for it. I can count the famous people I know on one hand.'

She borrowed a mug from beside the coffeepot so that she could take Rapunzel a cup of water. The chequers game was underway, and even those of the coffee crowd who weren't playing were watching in intense silence.

'Have you quit drinking coffee?' Ross asked.

'Not at all, this is for Rapunzel. Come on back to the stockroom and see what I found this morning.'

He groaned, but he followed her. 'If we have half-a-dozen replicas of that cat, I'm going to——'

'Only one,' Kelly assured him.

'One kitten? I'll be darned.' He peered down into the box. 'Can't you count, Kelly Green?'

'Well, you were talking about replicas, and only one of them looks like Rapunzel,' Kelly said defensively.

The cat rose and stretched gracefully, ignoring the still-blind kittens who protested when their warmth and nourishment were suddenly removed, and came to sip daintily at her water.

Ross was eyeing the kittens, who were walking over each other in panic to reach their mother. Rapunzel finished her drink, rubbed briefly against Kelly's hand as if to say, 'Didn't I do a good job?' and returned to the box. The squalls died as the kittens settled back into comfort.

'Maybe we can use them as an advertising gimmick,' he said. 'Give them away as prizes in a contest——'

'Give them away?' Kelly's spine straightened in shock. 'I couldn't bear to give them away,' she said. 'They're sweet!'

He eyed her in pained silence, and finally said, 'If the bookstore doesn't take off, you may have to go into the pet business. With Rapunzel around, you'll always have an assured supply of kittens.'

'Ross, don't be inhuman.'

'I'm not, just factual. Are you going to stay here and play with the kittens?'

'They're too little to play with.'

'Good. Then maybe we can get some work done.'

She stayed there for another minute, watching Rapunzel, who was curled around her kittens. All three of them were half-asleep. 'Look,' she told the cat softly, 'the babies are adorable. But no more, do you hear me? Patrick might not have cared, but I know all about the over-population problem in the pet world, and three cats is all that I can handle.' Rapunzel looked at her reproachfully and started to bathe one of the kittens.

'Nevertheless,' Kelly told her, 'as soon as the kittens are old enough, we'll see what the veterinarian has to say about you——'

Then she heard Ross say cheerfully. 'Good morning, Mr Olsen,' and she was on her feet and back to the store before she was even conscious of having moved.

What was the owner of the University Bookstore doing here, she wondered. Surely by now it should be obvious to him that they weren't going to sell out!

She leaned on the counter, trying to look casual as she flipped through the books that she had stacked there, but she was listening intently to the conversation that was going on just a few feet away.

Olsen gave the store an appraising glance. 'This place sure looks different to the way it did when Patrick was running it,' he observed.

'Give us credit for a few new ideas,' she snapped.

'Kelly——' Ross groaned.

Olsen looked at her, then turned back to Ross with a raised eyebrow. Ross said, as if he were forcing himself to be polite, 'Kelly and I are partners.'

Olsen started to smile. 'And having a vile time of it, too, I see,' he said silkily. 'Tell me, Clayton, after a week in the business, have you changed your mind? The hours are atrocious, the profit margin is thin——' He glanced around, and corrected himself. 'In this store, the profit margin will be invisible, because your location is all wrong. If you were downtown, you might stand a fighting chance.'

Kelly stared at him, her green eyes cold. 'Tell me, Mr Olsen,' she said, 'why are you here? Did you come in to give us the benefit of your years of experience, or is there another reason?'

He smiled. 'Diplomacy, my dear,' he recommended, 'and tact. Learn those, and with a face and figure like yours you could go a long way. But as it is——'

'I'll thank you to cut out the personal comments,' Kelly snapped.

Ross had turned to look at her, too, and his eyes were travelling over Kelly as though he'd never quite seen her before. Then, almost reluctantly, he turned back to Olsen. 'You said when you first came in this morning, that you had a proposition for me,' he reminded.

'I'm making another offer to buy you out,' Olsen said, with an expansive gesture that took in the entire store. 'I'll give you a modest profit on the new stock; it will save you the trouble of returning it all to the distributors. And as for the old books—shall we say two thousand dollars for the lot?'

That's double his last offer, Kelly thought. But we've sold half the books that were on the shelves at the start of the week. Why does he want them badly enough to offer twice the money for half the books?—especially after they've been picked over by so many people?

Ross was staring at her, the expression in his eyes warning her to be quiet. 'We'll consider it,' he said. 'That seems a generous offer, and frankly, I'm not fond of the hours we're spending here. But we have gone to a lot of trouble and expense to restock the store. It hardly seems right to close down so soon.'

'Why throw good money after bad?' Olsen asked reasonably. 'I know what you've spent on advertising this week, and I'll pay a fair price for your new stock.'

We must be hurting his business, Kelly thought, and had to fight to keep a triumphant smile off her face. We've made the first dent, and he doesn't want to have to fight the competition. He wants us out of business before the semester ends and the students over at the college want to turn in their books. Olsen is no fool.

'You think it over, Clayton, and let me know—shall we say, by Monday?' Olsen was smiling. 'Last time we didn't set a date, and the next thing I knew you were open for business. I'd like a definite answer this time.'

Kelly said, 'The answer is——'

'That we'll have to talk it over,' Ross interrupted firmly, with a glare at Kelly.

'Whatever you say. By the way, I'm having a party tonight, if you'd like to forget the hostilities for a while and come over.' Olsen tipped his hat and started for the door. Then he paused, and went across to the chequer players. 'You still play a good game, Mr Keswick,' he said to Joe. 'I'd like to take you on myself some time.'

With a crooked smile at Kelly, he went out.

She released the breath that she had been holding, and turned on Ross. 'Why didn't you tell that arrogant, oily so-and-so to drop dead?' Kelly snapped. 'You made it sound as if we were ready to give up——'

'I don't know about you, but the pleasures of retail trade are already palling for me. Sixteen-hour days are wearing me down.'

'And you aren't even sorting the books,' Kelly complained. 'All you've been doing is flirting with the female customers——'

'And setting up a bookkeeping system, and keeping the inventory straight,' he pointed out.

'With the help of your friend, who's probably doing all the work, if the truth was known——'

'While you have been in the stockroom drinking coffee and playing with the cats.'

'Playing with——' Kelly was furious. 'You certainly were no help at cleaning up the mess Patrick left that room in. And——'

They were face to face across the counter, and both of them were furious. 'You're the one who forced us into this experiment,' Ross went on. 'You said you wanted to run this store all by your little self. Just where would you be if I hadn't decided to stay here and supervise?'

'Probably a lot better off,' Kelly shot back. 'All I hear from you is why I can't do anything right——'

He ignored the interruption. 'You'd have dropped from exhaustion by now. I know how tired you were last night——'

'Excuse me.' It was a polite but assertive woman's voice, cultured, a little prim. 'Are you Kelly Sheridan?'

They both turned in surprise to face a woman dressed in an elegant lavender coat with a matching hat. Kelly blinked in surprise, and finally stammered, 'Yes. May I help you?'

'I thought for a moment I had the wrong place,' the woman said softly. 'I was told, you see, that you ran a bookstore here—and it certainly sounded more like a fishmarket when I came in.'

Kelly gulped. 'I'm sorry. My partner and I don't always agree, and——'

Ross made a gesture, as if he'd like to take her by the throat. 'Ma'am——'

The woman ignored him, and answered Kelly. 'That's obvious.' She ran a disapproving eye over Kelly's sweater and slacks. It was apparent that she was not pleasantly impressed by anything she'd seen inside the store this morning.

Kelly took a deep breath and started over. 'Is there something I could show you?'

'The only reason I'm here at all,' the woman said, 'is

because my son asked me to stop and meet you. He assured me that I would be—let me see if I can remember how he phrased it—captivated by your sweetness.'

'You're Allen's mother?' Kelly whispered. And Ross had chosen that very instant to start a fight! The man was a jinx, she thought bitterly.

'Yes, I'm Mrs Parrish.' The woman took a tighter grip on her handbag, as if it might be snatched from her hand. 'I told him I'd invite you to meet the rest of the family, and we certainly will do that.' There was a brief pause. 'Some day,' she added, and it was like a door slamming in Kelly's face. 'It was so—interesting—to make your acquaintance, Miss Sheridan.'

Mrs Parrish was gone before Kelly could find her voice. She put a hand over her eyes, and then decided not to give in to tears in front of Ross. It was his fault, after all. She wheeled around from the counter and said, 'Damn you, Ross Clayton! You had to go mess that up for me, too, didn't you? You're so determined to get your own way——'

'How was I to know who she was? And if you'll be halfway honest, Kelly, you have to admit it was you who started the fight.'

'Oh, I did, did I?' Her voice was rising. Across the room, the chequers game had come to a halt, and the coffee crowd was watching this new entertainment with interest.

'We are being observed,' Ross pointed out.

Kelly was too furious to care. 'I started it, you say? Well, who was so pleasant and charming to that snake-oil salesman, and told him we'd think about his generous offer? I'm so furious I could kill——'

'Murdering me would solve your problems,' Ross agreed. 'One of them, at least. But somehow I doubt that Mrs Parrish would bail you out to come to dinner. Look, Kelly Green——'

'Don't you call me that!' she stormed.

He sighed. 'All right. But would you go cool off? Go take a nap. Go for a walk. Have a cold shower. Just get out of here for a while, and maybe then you can come back and be pleasant.

'Pleasant?' Her voice was rising. 'I am always pleasant! You are the only thing on this earth that makes me unpleasant!'

He was guiding her towards the stairs. 'Fine. Just go and be pleasant upstairs for a while. Alone. It will give us both a rest.'

She shook his hand off her arm. 'Stop treating me like a child!'

'Do you mean this isn't a temper tantrum?'

'Oh, I know what you're up to. You aren't fooling me! You want me to leave so you can throw it in my face later that I can't work the hours, that I can't stand the pace. Well, I can stand it! This is my business, and I'll run it.'

His fingers tapped gently on the iron railing of the spiral staircase. She was fairly certain that he would like to double up his fist and hit her. Then he shook his head reluctantly, as if denying himself the pleasure, and made a courtly bow. 'Then I'll go,' he said politely. 'Goodbye!'

But he didn't go up the stairs. He went to the back door instead, and a couple of minutes later the dark blue sports car streaked by the front windows.

Kelly sat down on the bottom step, as if all the breath had suddenly gone out of her. She had won. He was gone, and if she was lucky, he might never come back.

But would the victory be worth the price?

CHAPTER SIX

HE didn't come back all day. 'I'm glad,' she told herself stoutly in the middle of the afternoon, as she poured her twelfth cup of coffee. 'I can do my job better without all of his interference.'

She had the order book straightened out by then, except for a couple of special books that she had to ask him about. And the bills were paid, all the envelopes stamped and neatly piled, ready to be posted on Monday. Trade had slacked off, and most of the customers just wanted to browse, but Kelly had made a couple of good sales. The total on the register wouldn't be overwhelming, but it would do. It would at least show Ross that she could do it herself, she thought, and raised her chin defiantly.

Then it grew dark. No amount of light could penetrate the gloom in the corners of the big room. The stacks of books cast eerie shadows, and the quiet was enough to set Kelly's nerves on edge. Every time the old building creaked, she jumped. There was only a trickle of customers now, and sometimes for long minutes she was alone in the store.

What would I do if a robber came in? she wondered. Or if some shifty-eyed character appeared, and threatened me? Anyone walking by on the street can see I'm alone in here, and if he wanted to pop in and commit murder——

'Oh, stop it,' she told herself aloud. It was silly to let herself get scared out of her mind over a simple thing like working late in the store. It would be a part of her life from now on, and the sooner she got used to it, the better. Ross wouldn't always be upstairs to rescue her if she pushed the panic button. She'd better adjust her thinking, and start taking care of herself. She wished, though, that she had brought down another box or two of books from her room. She might as well be sorting books as be sitting here letting her thoughts roam idle, that was certain. She sat down in front of the fireplace, and concentrated on the flickering flames.

'Business is slow tonight,' Joe Keswick observed. He came down the spiral stairs, slowly, being careful of each iron step. Kelly sympathised with his caution; she'd taken the stairs at a run once and still had a yellowing bruise on her knee to prove it.

'After this week, the store won't be open quite so late,' Kelly said. 'Everybody must be at the movies tonight, or out to dinner, or just staying home.'

Joe took the rocking chair across from hers. 'Doesn't make sense,' he observed. 'Pretty girl like you, sitting here on a Saturday night. You should be out dancing.'

'Dancing,' she mused, still watching the fire. 'Is that what you used to do, Joe?'

He grinned. 'Yeah. Every Saturday night. I was quite a high-stepper in my day.' He shifted in his chair, and pain flashed across his face. 'That was before arthritis and rheumatism, of course. Now I couldn't do a fox-trot if the fox himself was after me, but in the old days . . .' His voice was soft and reminiscent, with the faint brogue that crept into it sometimes.

Patrick's voice had been like that too, Kelly thought. How she missed hearing him call her name! 'I never learned to fox-trot,' she mused. 'Somehow, I feel as if I missed something.'

'The first good day I have, I'll teach you,' he promised. 'Kelly—I've been meaning to ask you something.'

He sounded serious. She looked up at him quizzically.

'About the building,' he said. 'Your lease is up in July, and——'

'I'd like to renew it, of course,' she said. 'If you want to raise the rent, I understand.'

'It's not that,' he said. 'It's—well, the building is getting a little beyond me, if you know what I mean.'

Kelly frowned a little. 'No, I'm afraid I don't.'

He sighed. 'I'm over seventy, Kelly. I've got a chance to move into one of those special apartments for old codgers like me—where they furnish everything.'

'Oh,' she said. 'And if the heat goes off, you call the superintendent, and he takes care of fixing the furnace.'

'Right. I'm getting too old to be tinkering with such things. I'm thinking I'd like to move, Kelly. And since you've already got the bookstore—would you maybe buy the building?'

'Oh.' She laughed a little. 'I'd love to own the building, Joe. It's just that I don't have any money, and I'm not likely to have any by July.'

'What about the bank?' he questioned softly.

'Well, they've already lent me a tremendous sum to get the business back in shape. I don't think they'd like the idea of a mortgage, too.'

'I see.' There was a silence. 'Well, you can't blame a man for trying. The market's a bit limited in this neighbourhood. I guess that means I'll be staying, Kelly.'

She breathed a sigh of relief. 'I couldn't ask for a better landlord,' she said.

'Ah, it's an old building, but I take pride in it.' He rocked silently for a while, while he packed his pipe with tobacco and held a match to it.

'It's too bad,' Kelly said thoughtfully, 'that so many of the buildings in this area are empty. If someone would fix them up and start some little shops, we could have a whole district. A little village of craft stores and speciality shops——'

Joe puffed on his pipe. 'Don't look at me, young lady,' he said. 'I'm far too old to start a project like that.'

'And I'm far too poor,' Kelly laughed. 'I believe it's closing time, Joe.' She went to lock the front door.

'Where's the young man?'

'Oh, he hasn't come back yet.' It was said airily; there was no point in letting Joe guess that she had no idea where Ross had gone, or when—or if—to expect him.

Joe shook his head several times. 'Not a good sign, that.'

Kelly had gone into the stock room to check on Rapunzel and her family, and half-heard what he'd said as she came back out. 'What do you mean?'

'You should watch out. A good man doesn't run from a quarrel like that.' He nodded wisely to himself.

'But sometimes a wise one does.' She opened the cash register and started to count the contents.

'A man like that——' Joe said thoughtfully. 'You should watch out for him, Kelly Green. He's not a marryin' man.'

Now he's doing it too, she thought—calling me Kelly Green. Then the rest of what he had said hit her, and she started to laugh. 'Who cares if Ross is the kind to get married? We're partners, nothing else.'

'Never saw ordinary partners strike such sparks off each other,' Joe said wisely. 'Good night, Kelly.'

Ross didn't come back that night. Kelly fixed her supper, discovered that she was too tired to eat, and sat down to watch television for a few minutes, hoping it would quiet her mind and soothe her caffeine-jangled nerves so she could sleep. She woke a couple of hours later, coming from exhausted slumber to panicky alertness in the space of a split-second.

Ross is home, she told herself. That was the noise I heard.

But his apartment was still dark, and she finally went to bed, rubbing her neck, made stiff by the hard sofa pillows. At least the man could be considerate enough to tell her whether he intended to come back at all, she

thought irritably. But perhaps Ross himself didn't
know. Perhaps he had just gone aimlessly. Perhaps he
had gone back to Chicago—to Whitney . . .

And good for him, Kelly told herself crossly. She
punched at her pillow, wishing it was Ross. He deserved
to be stuck with a woman who led him a dance. Not the
marrying kind, was he? She should have told Joe all
about Ross and his hopeless love.

She'd done that at least fifteen times in her mind, with
every variation of expression, from pseudo-concern to
scorn, by the time morning broke. Sunday morning—her
first day off from the bookstore. And if it hadn't been for
Ross, she reminded herself, she might be spending the day
with the Parrish family, building friendships with the
people who would be her new family. Instead here she
was, alone, surrounded by work.

She carried a couple of boxes of books downstairs
and started to sort them out. Then rebellion rose strong
in her, and she reached for her jacket. If Ross didn't
come back, she might not have another day away from
the store in a long time—even Sundays would have to
be spent in keeping up with the bookwork and the
orders, the kind of thing he was so good at. But she was
damned if she'd sacrifice today as well! She'd have a
good time, and enjoy the spring air. This had always
been her favourite season, and she refused to be cheated
out of spring!

The grass was greening on the rolling hills of the little
cemetery as she dropped her bike on the gravelled path
and walked, puffing, over to Patrick's grave. 'I'm out of
shape,' she confided. 'There isn't much exercise in
carrying boxes of books around.'

She sat down cross-legged beside the marble
stone, and broke off the weeds that had already
sprung up beside it. The date of Patrick's death
was newly chiselled, and the outline of the num-
bers stood sparkling white, in contrast to the weathered
grey of the other lettering. Mr Bradford must have

taken care of it, she thought.

She sat there in the quiet for a few minutes, listening to the chirp of a robin somewhere nearby, letting the sunshine soak her tensions away. How lovely it would have been, she thought, if Patrick had lived, and if he had turned the operation of the bookstore over to her. But as it was, with Ross in the way——

'Your nephew is impossible, Patrick,' she said aloud. 'He's bossy, domineering, irritating, and I have a strong suspicion that he's trying to sell the bookstore from under me.'

It sounded even worse, when she said it right out in the open that way. She chewed on a blade of grass and thought about it. Patrick must not have known what kind of person his precious nephew had turned into, she decided finally. If he'd realised what kind of monster he was creating with that partnership, he would have reconsidered.

'And left me out of his will,' Kelly reminded herself. He wouldn't have disinherited Ross, his own flesh and blood. 'So quit moaning about it, Kelly,' she ordered. 'You could be a lot worse off.'

And if Ross had his way, she would be. She sighed and got up from the grass. The peacefulness of the little cemetery wasn't having its usual calming effect on her today. She'd stop at home and fix herself a picnic lunch and take it over to the park, she decided. It was too nice a day to be closed in anywhere.

The telephone was ringing in her apartment. Kelly debated with herself about answering it at all—it was probably someone who wanted her to open the bookstore. But it might be Ross, she thought, telling her what he had decided to do, so she answered it.

It was Allen instead. 'I thought Mom was going to invite you for dinner today,' he announced.

She finished spreading peanut butter on her sandwich and licked the excess off the knife. 'I don't think your mother was impressed,' she said.

'She told me that she couldn't understand why I thought you were—— Well, anyway, I'll ask her again. Once she understands how important it is to me——'

'I wouldn't bet on it.'

There was a brief silence. 'What in heaven's name did you do to her, Kelly?'

'Why do you automatically assume that it was I who did something?' Kelly was feeling discriminated against.

'Well, it certainly wasn't Mother.'

Kelly tapped her fingers on the telephone. 'Why don't you come over this afternoon and we'll talk it over?'

'Oh—I can't. I promised Mother I'd stick around here.'

'I see. Whenever you can fit me in, Allen—just let me know.'

She put the phone down with a bang and grabbed her sandwich. 'I'm going to find some peace and quiet before anyone else calls,' she fumed.

Every person in town, it seemed, felt the same way, and they had all gone to the park. Kelly found a secluded little spot to sit and eat her peanut butter sandwich, and then stayed on, leaning against a log, to watch the people. Every student at the university, it seemed, had decided to skip studying today to take advantage of the warm weather. Everywhere there were couples—jogging, playing like children on the swings, tossing a stick for a dog to retrieve. One young pair was simply walking in what looked like aimless circles, hand in hand, absorbed in each other. Only Kelly was alone.

I could have been with Allen today, Kelly told herself, and tried to work herself up into the fury at Ross that she'd felt yesterday. She couldn't do it. He'd been right; she had started the argument that Mrs Parrish had walked in on. And even if Kelly hadn't been the only cause of it, she had been right there with the catty remarks. It was no wonder the woman had been unimpressed, and Kelly could blame only herself.

She couldn't even blame Allen. It wasn't his fault that he had family obligations. He was the only son, and of course his parents wanted some of his time. I could have been there too, she reminded herself, if I'd only behaved like a lady yesterday.

She had wanted Allen's parents to like her. It would be hard, now, to overcome that first bad impression, and yet it was so dreadfully important. It wasn't just a matter of whether they got married soon or waited till Allen's graduation, either. If his parents didn't like her, it would be uncomfortable all the way around, married or not. And Allen would still have to work with his father . . .

It wouldn't have been easy, she knew, even without that scene yesterday in the bookstore. Allen's parents were prominent people; his father had been a city councilman, and Mrs Parrish was the acknowledged society leader in the whole town. It would take some doing to impress them, and Kelly Sheridan had neither the background, the money, nor the family to do so.

'Face facts,' she told herself firmly. 'You're just a small-town girl who never went to dancing lessons, much less finishing school. Your parents were ordinary people who managed to scrape together a living wage. They died poor, and it took every cent they had to get you through college. Not much of a recommendation to the Parrishes—with their grand house and their luxury cars!'

But her parents had enjoyed themselves, she thought rebelliously, which was more than Mrs Parrish appeared to do, despite her co-ordinated clothes and her professionally coiffed hair. Kelly's parents had loved each other, and they had loved her, the child they had never expected to have. 'They were nice,' Kelly muttered. 'They were polite. And they never, ever judged people before they met them. Which is more than Mrs High-and-Mighty Parrish can say!'

'The way you're muttering,' a lazy voice said from

behind her, 'you're obviously tearing someone's character apart. From past experience, I suspect it's me. A wise man, at this point, would just walk away and pretend he'd never been here——'

'Ross!' She twisted around against the log and looked up. From this perspective he seemed incredibly tall. The shock of seeing him here was unhinging her mind, she thought. She felt almost glad to see him, a little relieved that he hadn't just gone back to Chicago without letting her know. My mind is wearing out, she thought.

'However,' Ross went on, 'this just goes to prove that I'm not wise. May I?' He sat down next to her and leaned against the log. 'Did you miss me?'

'Of course not,' she said with perfect composure.

He grinned. 'That's what I thought. I missed you.'

'Is that why you came back?' Kelly asked tartly.

'Not altogether.'

'Where were you, anyway?'

'At a party.' He stretched his feet out and sighed comfortably.

Kelly began to smell a rat, and her initial happiness to see him began to fade. 'Mr Olsen's party?' she asked, warily.

'How'd you guess?'

'It seems the sort of underhanded thing you'd do. What are you doing, discussing selling the bookstore behind my back? Working out how to sabotage me——'

'Whoa!' His hand clamped on her shoulder, preventing her from jumping to her feet. 'Kelly Green, you have the fastest temper I've ever run into, and from now on, whenever you start to display it, I'm going to stop you.'

She thought about that one for a moment. 'How?' she asked tartly.

'You'll see. It's my resolution of the week.'

'If you want to talk about losing tempers, you can do a good job of getting angry too, you know.'

'I know. It got me stuck with you, didn't it?'

She bit her tongue. 'If I want to lose my temper——'

'Then you'll just have to take the consequences,' he finished amiably, and settled an arm comfortably around her shoulders. 'You should have gone last night.'

'To a party given by that slippery, low-down excuse for a man? I don't hang round with people like that.'

'You might have found out something interesting.'

'Like what?' she snapped. 'That you're still trying to make me give up the store? I already know that, and if you think for one minute, Ross Clayton, that you can force me to sell out——'

'There you go again,' he said sadly. 'With a temper like that, you should have been a redhead to match. And now for your first lesson, Kelly Green——' His arm was like a steel bar, drawing her close to his side.

'What do you think you're——'

He ignored her protest and kissed her, long and hard. Every drop of breath in her lungs seemed to vanish, absorbed by the shock that seemed to rock her to her toes. Defiantly, she kept her eyes open, staring up at him with malice.

Ross didn't seem to mind. He simply tightened his hold and kissed her again. This time the mere touch of his mouth scorched her delicate skin, and when he finally released her, she sagged weakly against him.

'Why did you do that?' It was a feeble croak.

Ross smiled. 'I'm just putting out the fire,' he said mildly. 'Every time you lose your temper, I'm going to kiss you. Eventually, you should become conditioned not to lose control any more——'

She was incensed. 'You sexist, chauvinist pig,' she snapped. 'How dare you put a hand on me to teach me anything?'

He raised one eyebrow and said sweetly, 'Are you asking for another lesson?'

Kelly swallowed hard. 'Don't touch me,' she warned.

'I already am touching you,' Ross pointed out. 'I still have my arm round you. Come to think of it, this idea could backfire.'

'How?' Kelly asked, sliding away from him.

'You might decide that you like to be kissed, and start losing your temper on purpose.'

'Me? Like to be kissed? By you?' Kelly shuddered delicately. 'If you've finished being absurd, Ross——'

'What's so silly about it?' He pulled her back against his side, and absently scratched his chin by rubbing it against her hair. 'There are a lot of girls——'

'Spare me the recital of your success with the ladies,' Kelly recommended tartly.

'All right,' he agreed amiably, 'I'll tell you about the famous author instead.'

'What famous author?'

'The one who was at Olsen's party last night. I told you that you should have been there.'

'What was a celebrity doing at Olsen's party?'

'She was knocking back Scotch on the rocks. Or were you asking why she was invited? I assume that Olsen is trying to talk her into appearing in his store as an advertising gimmick.'

'It figures,' Kelly grumbled. 'Which author?'

'Carol Phillips.'

Kelly whistled, a long, low, tuneless sound. 'The one who writes the steamy historical novels? Why is she wasting her time in this town?'

'The lady is here for a week or so, to give the aura of success to a seminar the university is holding.'

'And Olsen has her sewn up.'

Ross grinned. 'Not necessarily,' he said. 'I need to make a withdrawal from the cash register for expense money, by the way. She's having dinner tonight with me.'

Kelly blinked. 'You're joking! You pulled her out from under Olsen's nose?'

Ross said modestly, 'She doesn't think much of him, you understand. While I, with my infinite charm——'

'Compared to Olsen, your charm is outstanding,' Kelly admitted. 'Otherwise, it leaves something to be desired.' She smiled up at him, warmly. 'I haven't lost my temper, you understand—so don't get any ideas about punishing me.'

'Punishment,' he muttered. 'If the girls back home could see how you treat me . . .'

'So why don't you go back and collect the sympathy you're due?' Kelly asked sweetly. 'Do you really think you can convince Carol Phillips to promote our bookstore?'

'Why not? She doesn't have anything more exciting to do this week. She'll be bored to death inside three days.'

'Which means, because you're bored, you think she must be. If you miss the city so much, why don't you go back?'

He smiled down at her. 'Are you trying to get rid of me, Kelly Green? Wishful thinking, my dear.'

'And your job,' Kelly went on. 'Don't you miss your job? What do you do with the department stores, anyway? You never told me.'

Ross shrugged. 'I can barely remember; it's so long ago.'

'It's only been three weeks.'

'Really?' He looked fascinated. 'It must be only an illusion, then, that it's been an eternity since I met you in Mr Bradford's office that day.'

It was a good thing she didn't have a steak knife handy, Kelly told herself. She might have sunk it up to the handle in his chest, without a thought of what would happen to her.

Twenty minutes ago she'd been sitting there, half afraid that he would never come back, and frightened of whether she could make the bookstore a success without him. How foolish, she told herself. The man was, pure and simple, a troublemaker.

Ross said thoughtfully, 'To think that such a little thing as meeting you could ruin a man's whole life . . .'

She saw red, and then forced herself to bite her lip and smile. He wasn't worth losing her temper over, that was sure. And she certainly didn't want to give him any excuse to hand out more of those uncomfortable consequences that he apparently thought were funny!

CHAPTER SEVEN

THE Cornish hens were browning just right, and the wild rice stuffing was moist and delicious-looking. Kelly drew in a deep breath of the wonderful smell that filled her tiny kitchen, and basted the tiny birds again. The aroma was almost a meal in itself, she thought.

This evening was going to be perfect, she thought. Allen's birthday was tomorrow, and Kelly was determined that nothing was going to ruin this special dinner for him.

Not even the fact that law school final exams would be held the next week would be allowed to interrupt their evening together. Tiny lines cut between Kelly's eyebrows as she thought about exam week. She was going to try very hard to persuade Allen to put the books away for one evening and have fun. He'd do better on the tests, anyway, she thought, if he took a break from studying now and then.

'Now if I can just get Allen to believe that,' she told herself, and draped her apron over the back of a chair. Much as she would have liked to devote the rest of the afternoon to her menu, she did still have a bookstore to run, and a partner who was probably counting the minutes she'd been gone and holding each one against her.

'As if he was perfectly innocent,' Kelly told herself. Ross had spent every evening all week with Carol Phillips, ducking out of the store as early as he could each day in order to take the author to dinner, to the university theatre, to the concert hall——

'And he's spending company money to do it,' she added to herself. 'Some partner he is—he's spending it faster than I can bring it in.'

She came down the spiral stairs quietly so that she didn't disturb Allen, who was absorbed in a law book at the table in the back corner. He didn't even look up until she was standing beside him.

'Why don't you go upstairs to study?' she asked. 'It's even quieter up there.'

Allen shook his head. 'I just got all my books arranged so I can use them, and I don't want to move all this stuff again. I won't be able to study tomorrow, because Mother is giving a birthday dinner for me, so every minute is important tonight.'

Kelly bit her tongue. So much for her plans for a quiet, romantic evening for the two of them, she thought. With Ross gone and a bottle of champagne chilling in the refrigerator, she had hoped that they might even get around to talking about his parents, and their plans for the future . . .

'Sorry,' he said, seeing her frown. 'I asked Mother to invite you for dinner, but she didn't seem to hear me.'

'That figures.' She massaged the tense muscles at the base of his neck with her thumbs and made one more try at persuading him. 'Study hard, honey, so when the store closes, we can enjoy the rest of the evening. We haven't had any time together all week——'

He was shaking his head, already concentrating on the page again. She sighed.

Ross was straightening out the sale table, tagging injured books with lower prices. He had of course overheard the conversation, and he looked up at her with a gleam in his eyes that might have been sympathy. Or laughter, Kelly thought. Knowing Ross, it was probably the latter.

'That guy doesn't exactly make a girl feel like Cleopatra, does he?' Ross said, under his breath. 'If you'd roll yourself up in a rug to impress him, he'd trip over you and sue for damages.'

Kelly glared at him. 'Allen is a careful, conscientious——'

'Dull,' Ross supplied helpfully.

'Scrupulous student. And he's going to be an excellent lawyer, whatever you think.'

He looked surprised at the attack. 'I never said he wouldn't. I'm sure he'll be a good, dull lawyer. Is that really what you want to live with, day in and day out?'

Kelly said with dignity, 'I don't choose to discuss it with you, that's certain.'

'Very well. Do you mind if I leave a little early tonight?'

Typical, she thought. He had picked just enough of a quarrel to put her on the defensive, and then he said he'd like to leave early. He knew perfectly well that she would give anything right now to see the back of him.

'Of course not,' she said. 'Carol again, I presume?'

Ross grinned. 'Who else?'

'And what cultural wonderland have you discovered for her tonight?'

'I thought we'd catch the end of the track meet over at the stadium.'

'Track?' she repeated, in disbelief. 'You're taking one of the top-selling novelists in the country to watch a bunch of guys sweat while they see who can run the fastest around a circle?'

Ross shrugged. 'How much more excitement can you find in this town?'

'Oh, I don't know. It's certainly intriguing to watch the cash supply steadily disappear from the register into Carol Phillips' mouth, that's sure. How much can one woman eat?'

He looked a little uncomfortable. 'Part of that was flowers,' he said finally.

'Flowers? You're spending our hard-earned money on flowers for that woman?'

'She does have certain expectations, Kelly Green.'

'Well, I have expectations, too, and one of them is to get value for my money. I've never met this woman— much less got any return on what you're spending.'

'You will,' Ross promised. 'She'll be back in the fall to teach another seminar, and she's promised——'

'She has? Isn't that exciting. And how am I supposed to get her to keep this bargain? You won't be here to flatter her with flowers.'

Ross smiled. 'How do you know I won't be?' he asked genially.

Kelly set a book down with a thump. 'Don't you dare threaten me like that!' she said finally. 'You said you were taking a couple of months off from your job——'

'I did. I'm thinking of extending my leave of absence.'

She was speechless. Finally she shook her head. 'The truth is, you got fired, right?'

'No. It's just that my father always told me I'd never get rich by working for someone else. I've half a mind to stay here and really plunge into the book business.'

Kelly didn't believe a word of that tale. 'You were sacked for doing something outrageous,' she accused, 'and now you're going to inflict yourself permanently on me. I want to see your records. I want to talk to your boss——'

Allen sighed and slammed a book shut. 'It's awfully difficult to study with you two quarrelling,' he pointed out. 'Why don't you shake hands and shut up?'

'I'd rather shake hands with a rattlesnake!' Kelly told him.

Allen stacked his books noisily, banging them together. 'A little peace and quiet would be a good improvement around here,' he said, and climbed the spiral stairs towards Kelly's apartment.

'How long are we going to have to nursemaid him?' Ross retorted. 'This is not a library, it's a business—or at least it would be if you would run it that way.'

'What do you mean, Ross Clayton? You're the one who's spending our hard-earned cash buying flowers——'

'While you're buying things like this.' He pulled a small, thin volume from under the counter.

'Oh, *Sonnets From The Portuguese* finally came in. It's beautiful, isn't it, in the embossed leather?'

'Right. All six hundred copies are lovely.'

Kelly was silent. 'I ordered half a dozen,' she pointed out.

Ross nodded his head like an avenging angel. 'You certainly did. But you wrote the number in the column marked 'cases'. So instead of six books, we got six boxes of these things. They're back in the stockroom.'

'Oh.' Then, hopefully, 'Can we return them?'

'It was a closing-down sale, Kelly. Remember? That's why you got such a fantastic price.'

It was a good point. What was she going to do with all those books?

'We could mix up a batch of cement and build a planter out of them,' Ross suggested.

'They'll sell,' she said, with a certainty she didn't feel. 'I can give one to Allen for his birthday.'

Ross handed her the book and rang it up on the register. 'I hope you have a lot of poetic friends,' he said cheerfully. 'Do you mind if I leave now?'

'Oh—let me check on my dinner first, and then I can stay till closing time.' She paused, halfway up the stairs. 'Are you going to be out all evening?'

He grinned wolfishly. 'Why? Do you want to make plans?'

'I'd just like to know when to expect you. What do you and Carol do with all of your time, anyway?'

The grin turned into a leer. 'Research,' he said softly.

Kelly groaned and opened the door of her apartment. The aroma of the roasting hens washed over her in succulent waves. Allen looked up from his books with a sigh. 'Honestly, Kelly,' he said, 'a guy can't ever get anything done around here.'

'But it's your birthday, honey. Can't I at least do something nice for you?' She leaned over his chair and put her arms around him. 'Allen, we have a whole evening alone together. Let's please take advantage—— '

The raucous buzzer sounded, and she jumped. What on earth could Ross need, down in the store, that couldn't wait two minutes while she checked on the Cornish hens? She swore under her breath, peeked in the oven door, and dashed back down the stairs.

'Telephone for you,' he said as she reached the bottom.

'For heaven's sake, couldn't it wait?'

Ross raised an inquisitive eyebrow. 'I thought you were trying to impress Allen's mother with how reliable and prompt and responsible you were. Making her wait on the phone wouldn't be——'

She snatched the receiver from his hand.

'Besides,' he added genially, 'there is really nothing coincidental about it. Whenever I can't hear footsteps up there, I know it's time to break it up!'

She made a face at him. 'Mrs Parrish? I'm so sorry you had to wait for me.'

There was a genteel sniff from the other end of the line. Then Mrs Parrish said, 'It has always been our custom, Kelly, to invite our children's friends to their special birthday dinners. Allen wishes to have you as a guest tomorrow evening. Will you be able to come, or will your duties at the bookstore keep you from attending?'

You're hoping, aren't you, Kelly thought. You would love to have me turn you down. 'I'd be honoured, Mrs Parrish.'

There was a moment of silence, and then the woman said, 'Seven o'clock. I'll send Allen to pick you up, since I understand you don't have transportation.'

'I'd appreciate that, Mrs Parrish.' She put the phone down gently and then exploded. 'She talks about him as if he were six years old! Sending him to pick me up— inviting me to his special birthday dinner!'

'He's still her little boy,' Ross said mildly. He was balancing the cash register. 'And he will be till the day she dies.'

'Your mother doesn't check up on you,' Kelly pointed out.

'No. But then I'm ten years older than Allen—and self-supporting.' He looked down at the drawer and added doubtfully, 'Well, at least I'm supposed to be self-supporting.'

'If it wasn't for dinners and flowers——' Kelly pointed out. 'Have you ever thought about asking Carol to go Dutch?'

He drew himself up to his full height and looked down his nose at Kelly. 'I couldn't possibly do that.'

'Why on earth not?'

Ross grinned. 'Because my mother wouldn't approve,' he confided.

'Well, then send the next bill to your mother.' Kelly locked the front door.

'That's an original thought.' Ross was giving it careful consideration.

'Wait a minute. You let me pay for the spaghetti that night at Mamma Mia's,' she reminded.

'That was different. It was business.'

'And what is Carol Phillips?' She saw him start to smile, and added hastily, 'Don't tell me. I don't want to know.'

The Cornish hens were every bit as tasty as the recipe book had promised. Allen scooped up the last grains of wild rice from his plate and looked across at Kelly admiringly. 'I didn't know you could do this sort of thing.'

'To tell you the truth, I didn't either. I've never had a kitchen to myself before.'

'Maybe I should give up on getting Mother to ask you to dinner, and have you invite them here——' He looked around. 'Unfortunately, the surroundings wouldn't impress her, no matter what the menu was.'

'I can understand that.' Kelly had to subdue a shiver at the very thought of the Parrishes sitting stiffly on the mismatched chairs at her tiny kitchen table, eating anything at all. 'But I am working on cleaning out the mess. At any rate,' she said, sliding a wedge of apple pie on to a plate and setting it in front of him, 'I'm coming to your birthday dinner tomorrow.'

'Mother called you after all?' He looked startled.

'Yes. I'm on approval, I suppose.' She picked at the top crust of her pie and tried to laugh it off. 'I'll spend the day tomorrow boning up on my manners. I'd hate to use the wrong fork or anything.'

'That would be a disaster.' Allen pushed his empty pie plate aside and headed for the living-room, where his papers were spread on the coffee table. 'I'd better hit the books again.'

'But Allen——' Then she swallowed her protest. At least he was here; she wasn't alone in this tiny apartment. Just having his companionship was wonderful, whether he said a word or not. On the other hand, she reminded herself, her options for something to do were severely limited. She washed up the dishes, trying her best to be quiet. She couldn't help but see that with every click of china or clang of pans, Allen seemed to flinch.

I can't be any quieter, she told herself firmly. After all, I do have to breathe now and then.

She settled herself in the rocking chair and started to look through a box of clippings that Patrick had cut from newspapers and magazines. Most of them made no sense to her at all, and she finally put them aside with a sigh. Ross would have to look through them, she thought. He might recognise the people, or be able to deduce why these stories and photographs had been important to Patrick.

Allen looked up. 'That rocking chair squeaks,' he said uncompromisingly.

Kelly jumped, surprised by the sound of his voice. 'I'm sorry,' she said. 'I didn't realise——'

'The rhythmic squeaking is driving me crazy. Can you oil it or something?'

'No. But I can stop sitting in it.' She moved to the window seat and curled up, looking down at the quiet street. Not a single person was within sight, and only an occasional car came down this way. The last rays of the setting sun reflected off the windows of the empty storefront across the street, and Kelly sighed.

Olsen was right about one thing, she decided. The bookstore was in a bad location, and it would take constant advertising and promotions to keep people from forgetting about it. If it was easier to shop at Olsen's store, people would do it, unless she offered them bargain prices and special deals.

She looked across at the empty store with dislike. If one other shop would open in the area, it would make things much easier for both of them. But as it stood, she would have a fight on her hands just to survive here.

The telephone rang and she jumped up, intending to take the call on the extension in Ross's apartment so she didn't bother Allen.

He slammed his book and said, 'That does it! I'm going to the library so I can get some work done.'

Kelly was furious. She hadn't caused the interruption, that was certain, but he was treating her like a stupid child. She swallowed her anger and picked up the telephone beside the couch.

There was a momen't hesitation, and then the husky feminine voice on the other end of the line said firmly, 'I'd like to speak to Ross, please.'

And which one of the beauties was this? Kelly wondered. It couldn't be Carol; it wasn't his mother. That's hardly an exhaustive list of the women Ross knows, she told herself firmly, and wondered why she cared.

'He's out this evening,' she said politely. 'May I take a message?'

'Tell him Whitney called,' the husky voice said. 'It's very important that I talk to him tonight.'

So there really is a Whitney after all, Kelly thought.

And she wants Ross. With the combination of that sexy voice and the face in that sensual photograph, how could any ordinary woman compete?

And why, she asked herself crossly, would any ordinary woman want to? If the prize was Ross Clayton—who would even bother to play the game?

This was her chance, she thought. A perfect opportunity to get even with Ross. All she had to do was to say sweetly, 'Oh, didn't you know? He's spending the evening with Carol Phillips. You know— the best-selling author? I have no idea if he'll be home at all tonight.' Whitney would be furious.

And it would serve her right, Kelly thought. After all, to let the man come to this little town, without making any effort to keep him in the city, and then to expect him to be sitting by the telephone whenever she called— the woman deserved a little pain. She had dangled him on a string for months, or maybe years—how long had he waited for Whitney to get over the loss of her husband? Maybe a shock was just what Whitney needed to wake her up.

Wake her up to what, Kelly asked herself. To the wonderful things she's missing by not having Ross around all of the time?

Well, she told herself, if Whitney gets him to come back to Chicago, at least it would solve my problem! And I don't want to mess that up.

So, regretfully, she said, 'I don't know when he'll be back, Mrs——' He had never told her Whitney's last name, she realized.

'Lattimer,' the husky voice supplied.

'But I'll leave him a note to call you. Would you care to leave a number?'

'He knows it,' Whitney Lattimer said. 'I'm staying at the apartment.'

Whose apartment? Kelly wondered briefly. She had said it so calmly, as if there was only one. Did they share it when Ross was in the city, she wondered, and then reminded herself that it was certainly none of her business.

Allen was slamming books together in a fury. 'It's bad enough with the study conditions around here,' he said. 'Poor lighting and noise and that damned cat running through every fifteen minutes. But when you start becoming an answering service for the jerk who lives next door——'

'It's his phone as much as it is mine,' Kelly reminded. 'It was less expensive to put in one and share it.' She reached for his arm, trying to soothe his temper. 'I'm sorry, Allen. Why don't we sit down and relax together?'

He shook her hand off. 'Dammit, don't you understand how important these finals are? If I don't pull through with a good average, I might as well give the whole thing up.'

'But you'll do fine!'

'That isn't good enough. It had better be excellent, or my father won't come up with the tuition fees next year. He can't abide a mediocre lawyer, you know.'

Kelly sat down in the rocking chair. 'All I know is, getting yourself upset like this isn't going to help your grades,' she said softly.

'I don't get upset when I can concentrate,' Allen pointed out bluntly. He picked up the stack of books. 'But when you're putting on the pressure, Kelly, it's more than I can stand. I'll see you tomorrow.'

He disappeared down the back stairs, and she heard the slam of the alley door. Two minutes later Ross appeared on the stairs. He looked at Kelly's stormy face and then down the empty stairs, and mused, 'I see you're all alone. Is there trouble in paradise, my dear?'

'Not as much as there could have been if I'd told Whitney where you were,' she retorted, and thrust the message slip at him.

He looked at it and then up at her thoughtfully. 'Do you think it would have bothered her—that I was out with Carol?'

'I don't know,' Kelly snapped. 'And I don't care. But I wish I'd told her anyway!' She stamped off towards her bedroom.

'On the whole,' Ross mused, 'so do I.'

So, she thought as she slammed the door of her bedroom, not even Carol Phillips could blot out his memories of Whitney. The woman must be something special, Kelly thought, to have held a man like Ross in love with her while she married and lived with and lost another man. And then to keep him on the string after that——

Yes, Whitney Lattimer must be quite a woman. And why that should make Kelly feel like crying was beyond her.

It's Allen, she told herself. That accusation of his had been unfair, and uncalled for. She knew that by tomorrow he'd be sorry he'd said it. Finals week was a dreadful time, she knew, and as soon as it was over he'd be a different person. But it still hurt, to be blamed that way.

At any rate, here she was with a whole evening ahead of her, an evening she had planned to spend with the man she loved. Instead she had empty hours stretching out before her, and a next-door neighbour who would probably be in to torment her at any moment——

Just what was Ross doing home so early, anyway? she wondered. It was unheard of for him to leave Carol Phillips at this time of the evening. Or had she got tired of him? Ross was charming, but a celebrity could always find entertainment even in this little town. The track meet might have been the last straw.

I don't care what he does, she told herself. If she's dumped him, at least we can stop spending all that money!

She opened the wardrobe door to reach for a more comfortable sweater, and shuddered. Her clothes were compressed into a third of the space; the rest was taken up by boxes that Patrick had left there. There might be anything in that wardrobe, she told herself, and decided that tonight was as good a time as any to find out. She could work off some of her frustration by throwing things away.

Ross was in her kitchen when she went to get the wastebasket. He sniffed appreciatively and said, 'I was hoping you'd come out. That pie looks awfully good, you see, and I didn't have dessert. In fact, I really didn't have dinner unless you count a hot dog at the track meet——'

'Do you expect me to have any sympathy for you?' Then she relented. 'Eat the whole pie if you want.'

He put a slice on a plate and followed her back to her bedroom. She turned at the door and he almost ran into her.

'Ross,' she said politely, 'I moved to get away from room-mates. Stay out.'

'I thought you'd like to hear about Carol.'

'Why should I?'

'Because she'll be back the first week of September.' He made himself comfortable on her bed. 'And she'll be here in the store for tea and an autograph party that Saturday.'

'I'm thrilled.' Kelly started to remove boxes from the wardrobe.

'You should be. She told Olsen she wasn't interested in a party for him.'

'Really?' Her eyes widened over the box she held. 'How did you ever work that?'

'My consummate charm,' he said modestly, batting his eyes. 'We don't even have to pay her to appear. She'll do it—as they say—for love.'

It brought unpleasant suspicions to her mind. Just what did Carol Phillips have in mind? 'I don't believe you.'

'Well, Oliver might have had something to do with it, too,' Ross admitted. 'You know, my friend in the book department back home. He offered her a contract for an autograph party in every Tyler-Royale department store if she didn't co-operate with Olsen.'

Kelly stopped short. 'What kind of a hold do you have on that man?' she asked finally. 'He murdered someone and you know where he hid the body—right?'

'Kelly, you underestimate me,' he chided. He scraped up the last bite of apple pie and set the plate aside. 'Besides, what did he have to lose?'

'I'd think he'd be regretting giving you all of his trade secrets. Is that why you're home early?—the agreement is made?'

'Not exactly. The wind was a little chilly at the track meet, and Carol was feeling it.'

'Poor Carol,' she said, with false sympathy. 'Did you call Whitney? She said it was important.'

'If you're worried about the telephone bill, I kept it under five minutes.' He was lounging now, full length on her bed.

It felt strange, having him there. He looked so darned comfortable, with his hands behind his head, his eyes closed, that she felt an almost irresistible impulse to tickle his ribs and ruin that calm. Or, on the other hand, to just give up on the wardrobe and curl up beside him. She was so tired these days, and sleep was so hard to find at night—— What would it be like, she wondered vaguely, to lie there beside him, cradled in his arms . . .

CHAPTER EIGHT

AND that sort of thinking would only get her deeper into trouble, she thought. Just because she was mad with Allen was no reason to fool herself about Ross. He was still the same irritating, maddening stranger that he had always been. Why on earth she was wasting her time thinking about him was more than she could understand.

'The boyfriend was certainly in a hurry,' Ross said finally. He didn't even open his eyes. 'He almost knocked me down on the back stairs.'

Kelly didn't answer. She pulled another box from the closet. She'd work herself into exhaustion tonight, she decided, and then she could sleep, free of the worry about the store.

'The problem with Allen,' Ross said thoughtfully, 'is that he hasn't finished growing up yet.' He raised up on one elbow and finished, 'And when he does, you may not like what he turns out to be.'

'I'm so glad you're concerned about me,' she retorted. It wasn't fair, she thought, that she was so scared about whether the store would survive, and Ross was lying there without a care in the world, psychoanalysing Allen! It was his store, too, after all——

But then he had a job to go back to, if the Bookworm failed. While she would be back where she started, with the addition of a large bank loan to be repaid. I should have given in at the start, she thought moodily. He's going to win. I should have had more sense than to fight him over it.

'Of course I'm concerned about you,' he pointed out. 'It's apparent to anyone with eyes that you and Allen don't suit. If you insist on marrying him, you'll both be miserable.'

He was wrong, of course, about whether she and Allen would be happy together, but there was a little glow of happiness deep inside her anyway. He really cared whether she was happy or not! Her heart began to sing a tuneless song. Maybe Ross wasn't such a bad guy after all——

He seemed to read her mind. 'And I'd hate to see a man suffer like that,' he finished smoothly. 'It's inhuman.'

Kelly yanked the pillow from under his head and threw it at him. He twisted away and rolled off the bed in one swift movement, so quickly that she couldn't even dodge out of his way. 'It's time for another lesson in temper control, I see,' he said pleasantly.

Before she could read his intention, he had blocked her path to the door and was coming towards her, slowly, as if gauging whether she was a dangerous animal at bay.

She backed up, inch by inch, and her hand tightened into a fist. He saw the movement and shook his head. 'Naughty, naughty,' he said. 'We can't allow physical violence, now can we?' His hand shot out and clenched her wrist.

'Then what do you call this?' she retorted. 'You're not exactly going in for gentleness at the moment.' She struggled, trying to shake him off, but her slenderness was no match for his compact strength. He held her as easily as if she had been a toy, and laughed at her frustrated attempts to free herself.

'Brute,' she said finally, giving one last twist to her arm in an effort to pull away.

Ross smiled. Then, before her startled eyes, every muscle in his body seemed to collapse, and he fell back on the bed.

'Ross!' she cried. Panic edged her voice, and she scrambled on to the edge of the bed. Oh, my God, she thought. There's a man dying in my bed, and I don't know what to do!

'You called?' he asked cheerfully. Before she was aware of any movement, he had seized her, pulling her down so that she was sprawled on top of him, held so firmly by his arms and her own weight that she could not escape.

'You're not paralysed?' she asked weakly.

'What do you think?' His hand slid slowly up under her sweater to caress the silken skin of her back.

'I think I'd better get out of here,' she murmured. 'I don't like this.'

'Oh?' he asked quietly. 'They why don't you leave? I'm not holding you down.'

The intimacy of her position was making her breath come harshly and painfully. Her breasts forced against his chest with each intake of oxygen. She was helpless to move, and yet she had to admit that he was right. He was not holding her, or forcing her to remain there. But the paralysis that had seemed to threaten him was creeping relentlessly over her ... I can't move, she thought in panic.

His hands had stilled, as if he was waiting for her to make up her mind. The moments dragged by, and still she could not stir. Their bodies were like hot metal, pressed together into a weld.

This isn't a game any more, Kelly thought.

Ross uttered a little animal moan deep in his throat, and then Kelly found herself pinned to the bed by his weight, and glorying in the intimacy of his touch as he worshipped her body with his hands, with his lips.

This is what I was made to do, she told herself dreamily, and then all rational thought was gone as her body began to make demands of its own. She tugged at his shirt, impatient when the buttons would not yield.

I never knew, she thought, how powerful a woman can feel when she's in the arms of a man. If Allen had ever let himself go, and showed me that I could feel like this——

Allen. She had forgotten all about Allen.

It took every grain of strength she possessed to push Ross away, for every nerve fibre in her body was screaming a protest, wanting to stay in his arms. It would have been far easier to remove the thought of Allen from her mind, she admitted, horrified.

You're cheap, she accused herself harshly. She had found out abruptly, in those few minutes of uncontrolled intimacy, that she had a sensual side far stronger than she had ever suspected. She had enjoyed being held and touched. But to have made that stinging discovery in the arms of Ross Clayton, a man she detested——

My God, she thought, panicky. I'm some kind of maniac, to have almost slept with a man like Ross——

'What happened?' he asked. His voice was husky, as if it had been sandpapered. He touched her cheek, where a tear sparkled, with a gentle finger.

Kelly shuddered away from him. 'Don't touch me. You've done enough damage.'

He raised an eyebrow. 'Oh? I wasn't aware that I'd left any scars.' He let a gentle hand creep up her arm, over her shoulder blade, down her back.

Kelly shivered and pulled away. Don't fool yourself, she thought. He's only going after you right now because Carol Phillips turned him down. If she hadn't got tired of him, he'd be in her bed right now, and not yours.

Very slowly, as if reluctant to leave her, he pushed himself away. His hand lingered for a moment on the swell of her hip., and Kelly had to fight herself to stay calm under that warm caress.

He sighed. 'I assume you finally remembered the boyfriend,' he said.

'It's none of your business what I was thinking about.'

'It breaks my heart to disagree,' he parried, 'but when the woman in my arms goes from warm and willing to something straight out of a deep freeze in rather less than thirty seconds, it's certainly my business.'

Kelly couldn't argue with that. She refused to look up at him. Miserably, she said, 'I am engaged to him.'

'A mistake that could easily be remedied,' he pointed out. 'Allen is the worst excuse for a man that——'

She flared, 'He's brilliant, he's responsible, he's——'

'Also pompous and dull,' Ross pointed out. 'And he has no imagination. Why you think you could be happy spending your life with that idiot is beyond me.' He studied her with a speculative look that somehow made her feel as if she were a specimen under a microscope. 'Unless it's the money,' he said finally. 'He'll step into an established practice, and it must be worth a great deal.'

'Money is important,' she said sullenly. 'And in this town, there obviously aren't many ways to achieve it.'

There was a long silence. 'So why don't you go somewhere else?'

'This is my home. I have no desire to leave it.'

'I see. Is mony the only thing that matters to you?'

'Of course not, but when you haven't had any you must admit that it's important.'

There was a long silence. 'And, of course, Allen is here.'

'That's right.' It was defiant, almost a challenge.

'He also lacks a sense of humour, you know.' Ross reached out, as if half-consciously, to trace her profile with a gentle finger.

'That's not true. Allen has a wonderful time at parties——'

'But life isn't a series of parties. And a person who can't find anything to laugh about every day can get to be mighty dull.'

That was a hit. It wasn't as much fun to be alone with Allen as Kelly had expected it would be, but that was just because of finals coming up. And in any case, she told herself, she wasn't about to admit that to Ross.

'He's taking care of the future so we can both benefit. It's important to look further ahead than the next car payment, you know.'

He raised an eyebrow. 'Was that nasty crack aimed at me?' His hand shifted casually and began to stroke her hair. 'All work and no play makes a poor candidate for anything, especially a husband.'

With a supreme effort of will, Kelly sat up. 'And all play and no work is worse. How do you pay for that car, anyway? What do you do at Tyler-Royale?'

'Are you trying to change the subject, Kelly?'

'I think you're just a travelling salesman,' she announced, 'and you don't want to admit it.'

'They don't call them that any more,' Ross said. 'They're mobile representatives, I believe.'

'And you actually don't know what they're called?' When he didn't answer, she said, with a challenge in her voice, 'Do you mean it's worse than that? Your job, I mean.'

He put a hand over his eyes, as if to brush away tears. 'I wasn't going to tell you this, but——'

'But what?' she asked with foreboding.

'At the moment, they're trying to decide what to do with me. They took a poll among the staff, and half of them want to pay me to keep staying away.'

'It doesn't surprise me. You're not exactly at the top in anybody's popularity contest.'

He sounded wounded. 'I didn't think you'd kick a man when he's down, Kelly.'

'If you mind other people's business as you've tried to manage mine, I sympathise with them. Too bad they didn't give me a vote. Did you ever tell Whitney what you thought of her husband?'

'Now and then. Why do you ask?'

'I just wondered if she told you to go to hell, too.' She disappeared into the closet and tugged out another stack of boxes.

'She paid just about the same amount of attention to me that you do,' Ross admitted.

'Then comfort yourself with the idea that you've done everything possible to save young womanhood,'

Kelly recommended. She reached the last box and tugged it out of the back of the closet. 'There. that's everything.' She opened it and groaned. 'Books. I should have expected it.'

'What else? I don't think Patrick ever parted with one.' He pulled out a handful of books and then let them drop back into the box. 'I've got it! The Bookworm was only a front for a sophisticated gambling den. That's where Patrick made his real money——'

Kelly ignored him and plunged into another box. For a moment, she stared at the contents. 'Ross,' she said. 'We might have something here.'

The serious note in her voice made him pause.

'It's the only one I've found that was wrapped in tissue paper in a box all by itself——' Tension made her fingers clumsy as she tore at the delicate wrapping.

He helped to ease the volume from the paper, and then sighed in disappointment. 'It's only the family Bible.'

The leather-bound volume must have weighed ten pounds. 'You have quite a family,' Kelly wise-cracked, 'to need all that room to list them.'

'You have no idea,' Ross said. 'I certainly don't know why he left the darned thing to me—I haven't the vaguest notion how many cousins I have, and I don't care.'

'Perhaps that's why,' Kelly retorted. 'Partick thought you should care.' She touched the embossed leather binding and carefully raised the padded cover to peek inside. 'I wonder how old it is,' she asked softly.

'Be my guest.' Ross relinquished the book with no sign of regret. 'I wonder what else he hid in here.'

She was turning pages gently. 'No wonder he wrapped it up,' she said. 'The paper is so fragile that the pages would crumble with use. This thing ought to be put in a museum somewhere, Ross.'

He looked up, with sudden interest. 'You don't

suppose it is worth something, do you?' he asked.
'Patrick was a sentimental soul, but it's possible that he
saved it for more reasons than just because the family
was listed here.'

'He would have known,' Kelly said thoughtfully. She
looked down at the elaborate leather cover. 'The
workmanship alone makes it fascinating,' she pointed
out. 'But surely he would have told you, wouldn't he?'

He had reached for the telephone. 'Let's see if my
friend the bookstore manager is at home.'

'At this hour? Be serious, Ross.'

'I am. Quite serious. Oliver won't mind.'

The book seemed to separate in the centre, opening
automatically to the family section. 'Look at the
penmanship in this thing,' Kelly exclaimed. 'I've never
seen anything so elaborate.' The faded ink strained her
eyes, and the exotic whirls and flourishes of the writing
made it difficult to recognise the letters. The lines were
closely written, in varying hands, inks and styles.

Ross put the phone down. 'No answer. I'll try him
tomorrow at work.'

'Figuring this out would take a year,' Kelly
complained. 'This spindly little writing runs from
margin to margin.'

'I told you I had a lot of cousins.' Ross seemed to
have lost interest in the book. He was headfirst into
another box, and suddenly he let out a whistle that
made Kelly jump and almost drop the Bible. 'You've
discovered Patrick's treasure cupboard,' he said, and
came up with a teapot on legs. 'And you've been
throwing your clothes into it——'

'My silver service!' she exclaimed, snatching it from
his hand.

'Is that what it is? It looks more like battered gold to
me.'

'That's just the tarnish.' She balanced the pot in her
hand, feeling the silver warm quickly to her touch.
'What else is there?'

'Take it easy, Kelly.'

'I can't. I never could stand to open one gift at a time at Christmas, either. I always wanted to tear them all open at once.' She set the Bible aside and plunged into the box, scattering papers in all directions.

Ross grinned at her. 'Thereby creating an even bigger mess,' he said. He unwrapped the sugar bowl and handed it over.

Five minutes later, Kelly was sitting cross-legged on the floor beside her bed, feasting her eyes on the largest, most elaborate tea service that she had ever seen. The engraved tray was three feet long and stood on carved legs. The hot-water urn had its own warming burner and pivoted on its stand to make pouring easy. The teapot that she had at first thought would be the largest of the pieces looked quite small in comparison. The cream jug would hold a full pint.

A far cry from the simple thing she had expected, from the description in Patrick's will. She sighed in gleeful contentment. What an addition this would make, she thought, to her first home! She couldn't wait to show it to Allen.

'I'll leave you to gloat over your new toy,' Ross said. He tucked the family Bible carefully under his arm.

Kelly looked up in sudden shock. He didn't exactly sound jealous, she thought, and yet—— It was a picture in contrasts, the worn old book he held, next to the precious silver. Tarnished though it was, the discolouration could not hide the beautiful craftsmanship of the tea service.

'He should have left this to you,' she said, finally.

Ross gave her a twisted smile. 'Somehow I can't see myself giving many tea parties.'

She sighed again, unhappily this time, and sat back. 'If you want it—after all, it belonged to your great-grandmother, not mine.'

'And her maiden name, as you might have noticed in the family Bible,' Ross said, 'was Kathleen Kelly.

Which tells you something about how Patrick's mind worked.'

Her finger traced the initial monogrammed on the tray. Yes, she thought, it was a K. 'But——'

'Besides,' Ross added, 'If you remember, I am not totally without expectations. I still get the bone china—whenever we find ìt. See you in the morning.'

She found herself polishing silver in her dreams, wanting to know how the set would look once it was clean and shiny, and woke exhausted. 'At least I wasn't worrying about the dinner party for Allen's birthday tonight,' she told herself, 'or about the store, for a change.'

She started down the steps, and then went back for the silver cream jug, a rag, and the polish. She felt a little sheepish about it, but if it was a slow day she might as well be doing something.

Ross was already downstairs. He didn't look much better than Kelly felt. There were dark shadows under his eyes, something she had never seen there before. Was it worry about Whitney? Kelly wondered. It was funny, she thought, how when you yourself were in love, it was easy to be concerned about others. It didn't look as if Ross's dreams had gone smoothly at all.

'You look awful,' she told him.

'Thanks. Blame it on your cat.'

Kelly set the pitcher carefully on a shelf in the stock room. She picked up the feather duster and flicked it over the cash register. 'Why is she always my cat whenever she's done something you don't like?'

'Because I'm convinced that you put her up to it. She moved her kittens again last night.'

'Why is that so awful?'

'They ended up on my pillow.'

'Oh.' Kelly tried to think of something soothing. 'You could have used the other pillow. It's a double bed.'

'I tried. And I woke up a little while ago with a stiff neck and three cats staring balefully at me, as if I was the one who invaded their territory.'

'Oh, the kittens' eyes are open!' Kelly was delighted.

'No, it just felt as there were six accusing eyes boring through me. I should have known,' Ross grumbled. 'I should never have got involved with a woman named Kelly. I should have remembered what happened to my great-grandfather when he made the same mistake!'

'What happened?'

'He had to put up with Patrick for a lifetime, that's what. Of course, that would have been a picnic compared to what I'm going through.'

She decided to ignore him. Of course his feelings were wounded, the poor dear. Nothing was going the way Ross wanted it to. She brushed the duster across the mantel. 'What are we going to name the kittens?' she asked.

'How about Hellfire and Damnation?'

'Ross, that's not nice. Besides, you couldn't stand out on the front step calling for them. It would offend the neighbours.'

'So who would be calling them?' He rubbed his neck. 'Certainly not me. And speaking of calling people—I caught Oliver at home this morning.'

For the first time she saw the Bible that lay underneath the counter.

'What did he say?' she asked eagerly. 'Is it rare?

'I couldn't be so lucky. Quite common, he said, with a few unusual features. It's worth a couple of hundred dollars, tops.'

'I wouldn't exactly call that common,' Kelly disagreed. 'But I'm sure you're relieved.'

Ross blinked. 'Why?'

'Just think! If it had been worth thousands, you would have had to decide whether to convert it into cash or keep it. Aren't you glad you don't have to make that choice?'

He looked thoughtful. 'I suppose you're right. I asked him about your tea service, by the way.'

'Oh? Is this guy an authority on everything?'

'Not quite. He thought, from my description, that it was probably worth five grand or so.'

'Oh.' Kelly's voice was small. She hadn't considered that the tea service would have a monetary value. She had only thought of the beauty of it, of the sensual pleasure of the silky silver against her fingertips. But five thousand dollars—that would go a long way towards paying back that bank loan, or towards buying security for the Bookworm. Should she sacrifice the silver for the good of the bookstore? She bit her lip and set herself to dusting every shelf in the place.

It wasn't until she heard Joe Keswick's creaky 'Good morning' that she realized he hadn't been waiting in front of the fireplace that morning as he usually did. It gave her a little jolt. Joe was, after all, well into his seventies. What if some day he didn't come downstairs at all?

He poured himself a cup of coffee and dropped a dime into the piggy bank with a flourish, so that Kelly was bound to see. 'Glad to see you two are talking to each other today,' he observed, limping across the store towards them. 'I got somethin' to tell you.'

'I can't wait,' Ross muttered under his breath, and Kelly jabbed him with her elbow.

'Now don't come to blows,' Joe begged. 'It's nice to be able to talk to you both at once. I got a chance to sell the building,' he said cheerily.

Kelly's heart sank. The new owner might want the shop vacant, or the rent might be raised above her ability to pay . . .

But there was something about the glow of happiness in Joe's face that touched her. She could not burst his bubble.

'So you can go into your convenience apartment after all,' she said, with a smile. 'I'm happy for you, Joe. When?'

'Oh, nothing's firm yet. It'll be a while. Any case, you have a lease through July, and the new owner has already agreed to let you stay on.'

Obviously, Joe was certain that nothing more was needed. And Kelly knew that if the buyer was honest, Joe was probably right. But something about it didn't sound quite safe.

'Odd,' Ross mused. 'I wonder . . .'

'What?' she demanded.

He shook his head. 'It just seems strange to buy a building like this, without any obvious reason.'

'He just took a notion he liked this building, I guess,' Joe said.

'Curiouser and curiouser,' Ross muttered. 'You don't suppose . . .'

His eyes met Kelly's, and together they chorused, 'Olsen!'

Joe Keswick looked offended. 'You needn't think I'd sell me building to that skunk, now,' he said stiffly, and his brogue thickened. 'And what would he be wanting it for, anyway, him with the big store downtown?'

'It does seem an expensive way to put me out of business,' Kelly said. She thoughtfully dusted the last shelf. 'But I wouldn't put it past him.'

'Well, it isn't Olsen, so you can put your pretty head at rest,' Joe said. 'Ah, here come the fellas now.'

'It occurs to me,' Ross said, 'that Olsen is no dummy.'

'Yes,' Kelly said drearily. 'I'd thought of that.' She went hastily past him into the stock room to put the duster away.

Ross came in a few minutes later and settled himself on the edge of a table. Kelly looked up from the silver cream jug, feeling guilty, and started to put her rag away.

Ross dismissed the action with a gesture. 'You might as well be doing something,' he said. 'There's certainly no business this morning.' He was chewing thoughtfully on a strand of liquorice.

Kelly dipped her rag into the polish again and started to work on the discoloured patches that remained. It must have been years since the jug had been polished, she thought. The tarnish she had removed was like soot on her hands.

'I'm surprised Joe didn't ask us about the building,' Ross said finally.

'He did. I told him we couldn't afford it.'

'Well, that's true enough.' He sounded abstracted.

'I'm sure it doesn't bother you,' Kelly said bitterly. 'If we lose our lease, it means you won't have to wait six months to force me to sell out.'

'We could always move,' Ross pointed out.

'And where is the money coming from for that?' Kelly picked up a dry cloth and started to buff the silver to a shine. The metal took on a soft, blue-white glow.

I won't let him beat me, she thought. I won't just quit! That's what Ross expects, but I can sell the silver set and use the money to pay for the moving costs.

Part with the tea service, the first really pretty thing she had ever owned? She steeled herself against the ache in her throat. If it came to a choice between the silver and the bookstore, there could be no holding back. The bookstore would make a living for her.

But the silver was so pretty. For the first time, it occurred to her that Patrick must not have had any idea what it was worth. As it was, the tea service was worth as much as the rest of the estate put together! Surely if Patrick had known, he would have wanted the silver to go to Ross. He must have thought that it was a mere gallant gesture to leave it to a girl with his mother's name.

Ross caught the confusion on her face. 'What foul motives are you imagining now?' he asked with resignation.

She thought she would choke. 'The silver,' she said. 'Patrick couldn't have meant for me to have it——'

'He made it perfectly clear,' Ross said. 'Look, I didn't tell you what it was worth because I wanted to make you feel guilty——'

She started to cry. 'But that's just it,' she sobbed. 'Now that I know it's worth a fortune——'

'Five thousand dollars is not exactly a king's ransom,' Ross pointed out. 'And that was only a guess by someone who's never even seen the damned stuff. Kelly, would you stop blithering like an idiot over it?'

'An idiot, am I?' she sniffed. She brushed tears away, and left a dark streak of tarnish down her cheek. 'Because, unlike you, I don't want to cheat anyone?'

'Kelly, you're only making things worse,' he warned.

'If you'd wanted the bookstore, and I didn't, I wouldn't have tried to take your half of it away,' she accused.

'Kelly—— For heaven's sake, will you stop?' He tried to seize her hands.

By then she was weeping in earnest. She rubbed a fist across her eyes and said, 'I'm not like you, Ross.'

'I know, Kelly Green. How well I know.' There was a note in his voice that startled her. Was he laughing at her? She looked up at him, offended.

Suddenly the laughter was gone from his eyes, and she found herself clinging to him, never quite sure how she had got out of her chair and into his arms. He was kissing her with a barely restrained ferocity that should have panicked her. But, instead, she found herself standing on her toes, pressing her body tight against him, revelling in the strength with which he held her close. His fingers brushed against her breast, and the flicker of desire that shot through her was like a lightning bolt. He took her mouth again, urgent, demanding, until she surrendered to the pleas of her body and relaxed in his arms. She felt the muscles in his back tense under her hands, and then he held her just a little away from him and said, his voice harsh, 'This wasn't accidental, Kelly.'

She tried to get her breathing back to normal. 'I know,' she said finally. 'You planned it.'

'I didn't,' he said tautly.

'I don't know what you have in mind,' Kelly said. 'I don't understand what you're trying to prove——'

'Nothing,' he said, and let her go. He turned his back and put a hand to his head as if it was hurting.

She saw the dark prints on the back of his shirt, where her fingers had clung, and looked down at her tarnish-blackened hands as if they belonged to someone else.

'I was just trying to make you feel better,' Ross said.

'Thanks anyway.' Kelly's voice was bitter. 'That kind of help I don't need.'

'About the lease,' he said, 'leave it to me.'

I'm afraid to, she thought. This whole thing is just another way to make me feel worthless, out of control. I can make it work, despite what he says or does, she told herself firmly.

'I'm going to go and wash up,' she said firmly. 'You might want to change your shirt.'

In the bookstore, the chequer players were unevenly matched, and the bystanders had turned to conversation instead. Joe Keswick looked up as Kelly passed, and his smile froze on his face.

'Well, I never,' he said, and his eyes sparked with anger. 'A man who would treat a woman like that should be shot!'

Kelly felt a red flush creep up her cheeks. Was Joe psychic? she wondered for an instant. Could he tell, just by looking at her, what had happened there in the stock room? 'It's nothing, Joe, really,' she whispered.

'A shiner like that one, and you say it's nothing?' He leaned forward and touched the corner of her eye gently.

She twisted away from him and ran up the stairs. Her bathroom mirror confirmed what Joe had said, and she stared into it for a long moment, looking at the spot of tarnish which looked like the world's worst black eye. Then she clung to the side of the sink and laughed till her sides ached and the tears flowed painfully, leaving dark streaks on her skin.

This morning I'm in a clinch with my business partner, she thought, and tonight, I'm having dinner with my fiancé's parents! What kind of woman did that?

CHAPTER NINE

'CHEER up,' Ross said. 'Having dinner with the Parrishes will probably be no worse than being eaten alive by a nine-headed Gila monster.'

'Thanks for the encouragement.' Kelly poured herself another cup of coffee and added too much sugar. Her hands were shaking already, as the dinner hour approached, and Ross wasn't helping matters. His idea of humour was making her cringe.

She tried to study him covertly, wondering if the embarrassing scene back in the stock room that morning had only happened in her imagination. His equilibrium was undisturbed, that was sure. Or was it? There was a tiny frown between his eyes that she hadn't seen there before.

Don't take any credit for interfering with his peace of mind, she warned herself. That frown was probably only there because Ross was trying to figure out how to take advantage of the sale of the building to make her close the bookstore!

She nervously smoothed the lacy collar of her pale yellow dress. It made her hair, twisted into a careful knot at the back of her head, look even blonder. She had spent an hour this afternoon getting dressed, and she had discarded almost every outfit in her wardrode before settling on this. Now she was fretting over her decision. Was it too formal? Mrs Parrish hadn't specified her menu; what if they were broiling steaks on the patio? Or maybe the dress was too casual. Were floor-length dresses in or out this year? Kelly suddenly realised that she didn't know. It had never been a necessary part of her life before. What did people wear to a dinner party in this town, anyway?

'How do I look?' she asked finally. She didn't expect to like the answer, but at least the silence would be broken. 'Will I do?'

Ross propped an elbow on the countertop and rested his chin in his palm. 'You look like lemon custard,' he said finally, and added thoughtfully to himself, 'I wonder if Gila monsters like the taste of lemon custard?'

'Ross, you're not helping the situation with your stupid comments.'

'Then stop asking me stupid questions. Do you really expect me to take this seriously?'

'It's serious to me. These people are going to be very important to me.'

He shook his head. 'No, they aren't. You'll never marry Allen, you know.'

'What makes you the expert? Are you issuing predictions now, along with your other specialities?'

'No. It's pure, old-fashioned common sense—which, I regret to have to tell you, you are sadly lacking. How long have you been dating him?'

'A little over a year. Why?'

'It's perfectly clear. You were at the age when most young women get married and start families. You thought you wanted that, too, but actually you weren't ready to settle down. So you chose a man——' He frowned over the description, and changed it. 'You chose a person who was obviously not ready to be married—Allen.'

'Of course I want to be married——'

'Now, yes,' he agreed, 'a lot of things change in a year. But Allen didn't grow up with you.'

'Ross, that's ridiculous.'

'Is it?' he asked quietly. 'Kelly Green, do you really want a husband who lets you bully him?'

She was startled into speechlessness for an instant. 'I don't bully Allen——'

Ross grinned at her. 'Then why,' he asked softly, 'are

you going to dinner to meet his parents? It wasn't his idea, and it certainly wasn't his mama's.'

She took a deep breath. 'That's got nothing to do with it,' she said, and wished that she felt as certain as she sounded.

'Then try this one on for size. If you're perfectly happy with Allen, why are you having so much trouble staying away from me?'

She shifted her feet and wouldn't meet his eyes.

'Happily engaged women do not find themselves kissing another man twice a day.' His voice was quietly relentless.

'I am happy!' she argued. 'I am!'

'And it you were miserable, you'd be damned before you'd admit it,' he said. 'You're a strong-minded woman, Kelly. You aren't going to be happy with a dish-rag like Allen.'

She was incensed. 'How dare you call him a——'

'Strong-minded,' he repeated softly, as if he liked the phrase. 'How's that for finding a diplomatic way to tell you you're being stubborn?'

She folded her arms and refused to look at him. 'And when did you start on a new career as a marriage counsellor?'

He grinned cheekily. 'I've always done it as a sideline,' he confided. 'I've been telling people for years to stay away from marriage.'

He wouldn't be so quick to scorn it, she thought, if his lady love hadn't married the wrong man. It made her feel just a little sad, for Whitney and even for Ross himself. As if he deserved her concern, she told herself briskly. The sooner she got him to keep his fingers out of her business the better! The man was a self-important, meddling beast. And that, Kelly decided, was probably what Whitney had told him, too. It was exactly what he deserved.

He had crossed the room to her. 'Remember what I said tonight, Kelly Green. And ask yourself—is it love, or stubborness?' He punctuated the comment with the tip of his finger on the end of her nose. 'Do you really love him, or are you just holding on to something you don't want any more because you're too obstinate to let go of it?'

The jingle of the bell above the door told her that Allen had come in. Just in time to see that last gesture, too, she sighed to herself. Had Ross seen him coming? He seemed to have a devilish ability to do precisely the wrong thing whenever Allen was present.

She picked up her bag and the silky shawl that matched her dress. 'Have a pleasant evening, Ross,' she said sweetly.

'I shall,' he promised. 'I'll try not to fall asleep before closing time. And don't eat the peas with your fingers, Kelly Green.'

She bit her lip, hard. Just who did he think he was, anyway?

Allen took her arm. 'Some day I'm going to punch that guy on the nose,' he confided.

'Don't. He just has to have the parting shot, that's all.' Besides, she thought, if Allen tried, he'd probably never remember what hit him.

Allen's suit was well-tailored, but somehow the coat seemed to hang on him. He was so tall and thin, Kelly thought. She supposed that was what caused him to look just a little stooped. That, and too much studying. If he would put on just a little weight, she thought, he'd look much better.

At least, she told herself cheerfully, the fact that he was wearing a suit meant that she was properly dressed after all. Suddenly she felt much better. How silly it had been of her to listen to Ross, she thought. He was only trying to create trouble.

'Nice car,' she said, running a hand over the leather upholstery. It was a Cadillac convertible, and Allen had put the top down. She wished that she had a scarf to protect her hair; she could feel strands coming loose.

'Yeah. Dad special-ordered it. I think he's going into his second childhood, but if he likes it——' He sounded preoccupied.

'Are you all right, Allen?' she asked hesitantly.

He shrugged. 'It's just the tests that are bothering me. I'm falling behind on my study schedule.'

'Oh.' Her feeling of well-being started to dissipate. The last remnants of it vanished with a pop when he pulled the car into the garage at the back of the big Georgian house.

'Let's walk around front,' he said.

'We can just go in the back,' she said. 'It's closer, and——'

He shook his head. 'Mother's orders. All guests to the front door.'

Obviously I'm not going to be treated as family, Kelly thought. Well, we all have to start somewhere.

She did her hasty best to smooth the loose strands of hair back into the knot, while Allen tried to hang up her shawl. The silky thing kept sliding off a hanger and eventually earned an oath before he got it to stay put. This is not a good sign, Kelly thought.

'Mother and Dad will be in the drawing-room,' Allen said, gesturing.

The room was huge, and so sparsely furnished that it looked barren. It was painted a soft blue, which was picked up by the small rugs that lay over the polished hardwood floor. The furniture was antique, and even Kelly's inexperienced eyes could tell that there was nothing that didn't fit the period of the house.

It's cold, Kelly thought. It doesn't feel like a house at all; it's more like a museum.

Mrs Parrish sat stiffly upright in a wing-backed chair, her long skirt arranged carefully around her ankles. Her husband was standing by the fireplace, a glass in his hand. They both looked unhappy, as if they had been interrupted in the midst of a quarrel, and Mr Parrish raised his hand to his bow tie as if it was too tight.

Oh, no, Kelly thought. A dinner jacket and a formal gown? Did she do this on purpose, just to embarrass me?

'Miss Sheridan,' Allen's mother said. It sounded as if the words hurt her throat. 'Won't you sit down.'

'Thank you for inviting me,' Kelly said. She settled herself gingerly on the edge of a Chippendale chair.

'Have a drink, Miss Sheridan?' Mr Parrish sounded vaguely interested.

'Oh—yes, that would be fine.' Now what do I ask for, she thought in a panic.

'I can give you Madeira, Chablis, vermouth, sherry——'

She wished that she dared sneak a look at Allen, in the hope that he would give her a clue. 'Um—just a glass of wine, please.'

John Parrish's hand stopped in mid-motion. Mrs Parrish seemed to freeze. Allen uttered a strangled little sigh and muttered under his breath, 'Those are *all* wines, Kelly.'

If I lift up the corner of the rug, she thought, I wonder if I could crawl under it?

Mr Parrish handed her a stemmed glass. 'I think you'll like this,' he said. 'It has a pleasant little bouquet.' There was a glint of humour in his eyes, and Kelly smiled up at him as if he had just thrown her a lifeline.

Mrs Parrish had seen the glint too, and she froze her husband with a look. He retreated to the fireplace and stared at the blazing logs as if he was fascinated by the design of the flames.

Kelly sipped her wine and said, 'You have a lovely home.' On a scale of trite, she told herself, I have just hit a new low.

Mrs Parrish turned the comment over in her mind, as if considering whether it was worth replying to. Finally she said, 'Thank you.'

Kelly swallowed hard. 'It's unusual, isn't it? I've never seen a house quite like it.'

Mrs Parrish unbent a little. 'It's a replica of a mansion in Williamsburg, Virginia. Authentic, of course.'

'Of course.' Kelly tried to smile, but her lips hurt too much. She wished, suddenly, that Ross had been there. He would have seen the humour in this, and with one wisecrack under his breath he would have punctured Mrs Parrish's self-consequence and set Kelly to laughing . . .

Mrs Parrish put her empty glass aside. She sat bolt upright in the wing chair. The upholstery in the back of that chair will never wear out, Kelly thought irreverently.

'Another glass of wine, dear?' John Parrish asked politely.

'No, dear. You know quite well that one before dinner is my limit.'

Despite the endearments, Kelly thought she had never seen a couple who looked so ill at ease with one another.

A couple of aeon-long minutes passed in a stiff silence, and then a maid in a black uniform came to the door. 'Dinner is served, Ma'am,' she said, bobbing a curtsy.

Mrs Parrish showed no sign of having heard the girl. She waited until the maid had vanished, and then she stood up. Mr Parrish was beside her instantly, in response to that silent command. 'Allen will take you in to dinner, Miss Sheridan,' she said, and swept out on her husband's arm.

Kelly hung back. 'I'm sorry, Allen,' she whispered. 'I didn't mean to embarrass you.'

'For heaven's sake, Kelly, don't you know anything?' he hissed.

'I should have thought they'd be pleased I don't drink,' she retorted, trying to keep her voice low. 'You could have warned me.'

'It never occurred to me. Everybody in the world drinks.'

'Well, not everyone knows the catalogue of wines. And their clothes—I had no idea this would be so formal, Allen.'

'Oh, that's all right. Mother and Dad always dress for dinner, but they relaxed the rule for the occasion.'

'It's just as well,' Kelly admitted. 'I don't own anything formal.'

'That's what I told Mother.'

And why that remark should make her even angrier, Kelly didn't quite know.

He ushered her to the chair at his father's right hand and sat down across from her, sending her a quick, crooked grin of encouragement. But it didn't quite reach his eyes, and Kelly smothered a sigh. Obviously she was not doing well at all, but Allen didn't have to act as if he expected her to slurp her soup!

The dining-room was just as formal and barren as the drawing-room had been. The table was draped in white linen, and huge napkins in crystal holders lay beside each place. The centrepiece was of roses, and the heavy smell of the flowers soon began to wear on Kelly's nerves.

The maid set a glass bowl of vichyssoise before her. Kelly ate it, but she didn't taste anything. It might as well have been library paste for all she knew. One course followed another in what seemed to be an endurance contest, and the conversation progressed in small spurts.

We must look like a bunch of goldfish, Kelly thought. One of us produces an air bubble of conversation, and the others all study it and watch it and wait for it to reach the surface and break before anyone does anything about it.

And I, she thought wearily, am becoming a little deranged from the strain.

After each course, Mrs Parrish enquired ponderously if Kelly had liked it. By the time she asked, 'Did you enjoy the Shrimp Bordelaise?' Kelly had to bite her tongue to keep from exclaiming, 'Do you mean that was shrimp? Good heavens, Mrs Parrish, I thought you'd discovered a new way to disguise hamburger!'

But she retained her composure, and smiled, and said, certainly, she had enjoyed the shrimp.

Eventually the *Crème Brûlée* over unseasonal fresh strawberries had been served and eaten, and the battle of the dining-room was over.

'We'll have coffee in the drawing-room, Helga,' Mrs Parrish announced to the world at large.

The maid bobbed another curtsy and vanished. Mrs Parrish rose.

She's angry, Kelly thought. I might be inexperienced, and perhaps even ignorant, but she expected me to break, and she's angry that I'm still with her. She's absolutely furious that I didn't tip over my water glass, or use the wrong fork for my salad, or finish off my dessert wine and ask for more, or go off into tears of frustration . . .

Nevertheless, Kelly knew with a sinking feeling just how thin the ice was under her feet. One minor slip and she would be finished, and she was all too aware that danger could come from any direction.

The men rose, but Kelly was surprised when they stayed in the dining-room. Mrs Parrish raised a plucked eyebrow and said maliciously, 'The gentlemen will join us after they've had their brandy.'

A glass of wine before dinner, two during, and a brandy after? No wonder Allen had said he wouldn't be able to study tonight, she thought.

She was more careful when she entered the drawing room this time, choosing the wing-backed chair that matched Mrs Parrish's. One-upmanship is a game we women learn quickly, she thought.

Mrs Parrish immediately settled herself behind the silver coffee service with a proprietary little flounce. Kelly gave her points for the gesture. 'Cream or sugar?' she asked with icy politeness.

'Neither, thank you.'

Mrs Parrish passed her a demitasse cup. Kelly sipped it and winced. She'd forgotten that after-dinner coffee would of course be stronger than usual. Well, she'd drink it if it killed her; she certainly wouldn't pass it back to be corrected.

She crossed her legs elegantly and determined that she would remain silent except when she was spoken to.

Mrs Parrish poured her own coffee and said mildly, 'I was glad to see that Allen seemed to enjoy his dinner.'

Kelly thought about asking how she could tell, since he'd said nothing. But she merely nodded politely.

'He spends so much time on his—activities——' it was said with a sideways look at Kelly'—that he doesn't eat properly.'

Activities, meaning me? Kelly thought. Well, she's really out to lunch if she thinks Allen is spending all his time with me.

'I wish he would put on a few pounds,' Mrs Parrish fretted.

Even though Kelly herself had thought the same thing only hours before, she felt herself burning with fury. If he wasn't trying so hard to please his parents, perhaps Allen could slow down, she thought.

Mrs Parrish set her cup aside and leaned forward. 'You do understand, don't you, Miss Sheridan,' she said confidingly, 'why my husband and I cannot give our approval to this relationship between you and our son? Allen has been raised with certain standards, and there will be expectations of his wife.'

Kelly clenched her fist, under the delicate napkin in her lap.

'A girl with no family background, who runs a book-store in partnership with a—well, I'll be frank——'

'Please do,' Kelly said softly.

'—a young man of shady character, simply is not an appropriate choice for Allen.'

Kelly sipped her coffee and said sweetly, 'I'm sure you're too polite to mention the fact that I inherited the bookstore from an elderly man to whom I was not related.'

'Now that you bring it up,' Mrs Parrish said, 'it did of course enter into our discussion.' She set her cup aside and leaned forward. 'I don't mean to be offensive, young woman, but it becomes obvious very quickly that you simply do not suit in our family.'

That was just it, Kelly thought. The woman honestly didn't set out to be offensive—she simply was, just by her nature!

'I quite understand,' Kelly said softly. 'And I agree, Mrs Parrish, that we would not suit.'

The woman sat back with a gratified smile, the first Kelly had ever seen her display. For a moment, she almost leaned against the back of her chair. 'I knew you would be approachable,' she said. 'I told John it was just a matter of talking to you about it, and you would see. If there is anything that John or I can do for you, of course——'

The woman was positively chatty, Kelly thought, with distaste.

'And I do trust that you won't tell Allen about this little chat?' his mother continued. 'I think it would be much better for him if——'

'Mrs Parrish.' Kelly cut firmly across the torrent of words. 'I don't believe that I've agreed to anything.'

'But——' It would have been humorous, watching her sputter, if Kelly hadn't been so angry.

'I agree that we are not likely to get along together,' she continued. 'But don't you think Allen should be the one who decides which of us he wishes to live with?'

The drawing-room door opened to admit Allen and his father. Kelly set her cup aside and stood up. 'It's been so pleasant this evening,' she said, 'but I know that Allen has studying to do, and I really couldn't bear to keep him from it. Thank you so much for the wonderful dinner.

Allen, if you're ready to take me home?'

There was a demand under the soft honey of her voice, and Allen was backing his father's Cadillac down the drive before he found his voice. 'Why were you rude to my mother?' he asked, then.

Kelly was stunned. 'Rude? Me rude? I've never been treated so badly in my entire life——'

'Well, you knew she wasn't delighted by the idea. But instead of being charming and placating, you practically told her you wouldn't make any effort to please her.'

'Not until after she'd told me a great many things,' Kelly muttered. But there was obviously no point in trying to explain it to Allen just now. She'd wait until he'd had a chance to cool off. After finals were over they could talk about it, and she'd tell him what his mother had said.

And he still won't believe it, she told herself. She turned sideways on the leather seat and stared at him, at the horn-rimmed glasses, the curly dark hair already starting to thin at his temples, the stooped shoulders. An old proverb came to her: if you want to know what a woman will be like after she's married, look at her mother.

Allen looked a great deal like his father, she thought. And if the proverb held true with men as it so often did with women——

What was it Ross had said? Did she really want a husband she could bully? That was it. Was Allen's father meek because his wife was domineering, or had Mrs Parrish turned into a shrew because her husband didn't take a stand?

Kelly sucked in a deep breath. I don't want to be like that woman, she thought, but for the first time she felt a spark of sympathy for Mrs Parrish. It could happen to me, Kelly realised. If he refused to make decisions, I'd get to be more domineering every day, until I was just like her.

I'll think it over, she told herself. And after finals——

Do you really love him, or are you just holding on to something you don't want any more because you're too obstinate to let go of it?

Ross's words rang through her head, and she clapped her palms over her ears, trying to block out the sound of his voice.

But it's true, she thought. He was right. And better to be done with it now than to have it hanging over my head for another week.

'I think we should reconsider, Allen,' she said quietly. 'It isn't going to work, and we'd be wiser to forget it than to fight hopeless odds.'

'Mother will come round,' he said. But he didn't sound very sure of himself.

'To be honest,' Kelly said meditatively, 'if she showed up on my doorstep tomorrow with Enrico Caruso, and sang an operatic duet with him inviting me to join the family, I still wouldn't be convinced.'

He looked puzzled. 'Caruso is dead,' he pointed out finally.

'Nevertheless, I'll bet that he would come before your mother would give in.' She lost herself in pleasant thought for a moment, and then said, 'Allen, there isn't any point to this. Let's just drop the idea of getting married, all right?'

He parked the car in front of the bookstore. 'I don't understand,' he said finally.

'I'm not sure I can explain. I just don't think I want to be married soon.'

There was a long silence. 'Right after finals,' he said firmly, 'we need to talk about this. Get it all straightened out.'

He would let nothing interfere with finals. Kelly realised that she should have seen that coming.

'There's nothing more to say, Allen. If I had an engagement ring, I'd give it back. Since I don't have a diamond, what can I do to convince you that I mean what I'm saying?'

'Must we talk about this now?'

'I don't want to talk about it at all,' Kelly said. 'I have nothing more to say.' She opened the car door. 'I'm more grateful than I can say for the dinner tonight, Allen.'

He frowned. She sighed and decided not to try to explain. 'I'll see you around,' she said, and slammed the car door.

The bookstore was quiet and dark, only the dim lights of the display windows showing her the way to the spiral stairs. She climbed them slowly, feeling lonely, weary, frustrated. But deep in her heart there was peace, as well.

I owe Ross a thank you, she thought.

At the top of the stairs she paused, wondering why it was so quiet. Usually when she was out he would turn the stereo on, and whistle along with his favourite classical albums. It drove Kelly mad to hear it, but tonight she would even have welcomed that.

'Ross?' she called from the door.

The apartments were dark. Rapunzel stretched and yawned when Kelly turned on the lights, getting out of the basket full of magazines on the windowseat and coming across to investigate the intruder. The two kittens yowled in protest.

'You moved your family again, I see,' Kelly told her. 'Or did Ross evict you from his bedroom?' Rapunzel stropped herself against Kelly's leg and purred.

'Ross?' Kelly repeated. But she knew he wasn't there, and suddenly the weight of the tears she had refused to shed, and the dark apartment, and the loss of Allen, were too much to bear.

'Ross, I need you,' she said, through her tears. 'I depend on you——'

And then another phrase came to her lips. The words were unspoken, but they hung in the silent apartment.

Ross, I love you . . .

CHAPTER TEN

KELLY closed her eyes tightly, and told herself she was being a fool. 'You do not go from being engaged to one man, to being in love with another, in the space of a breath,' she lectured tartly.

Ross was maddening, exasperating, irritating. He was the most frustrating man she had ever met, and the only one on earth who could drive her to lose her temper by making a single wisecrack. She had never spent so much energy quarrelling with anyone——

'And I've never been so much alive as when I'm fighting with him,' she added, softly. She sat down, hard, on a straight chair at the little kitchen table. 'Or when he's kissing me . . .'

It hadn't happened overnight, she realised, the shock of this abrupt realisation still making her feel a little dizzy. She'd been fighting against her disillusionment with Allen since she had moved into the new apartment. 'Since I met Ross, actually,' she admitted aloud. Hearing the words only increased the ache. What a stupid thing to do—to plunge headlong into love with a man who not only wasn't particularly attracted to her, but who was in love with a girl back home!

'Dummy,' she told herself, without sympathy. 'You're a real loser in the love department, Kelly Sheridan.'

Maybe she was wrong, she thought, grasping at the idea with hope. Perhaps she was just so shocked by the idea of being alone again, of living without Allen, that she had seized on the nearest male automatically. After all, Ross was hardly loveable. He was opinionated, bossy—

'Also charming, gentle, caring, strong . . .' She broke off in the middle of a catalogue of his virtues. 'You sound ridiculous, Kelly,' she accused herself. As soon as she saw him again, she'd laugh at herself for this silly episode.

Wouldn't she? she asked, in a small voice.

And where was he, anyway? she wondered irritably. He could at least have left her a note——

Now she was acting as if the man was married to her, she realised. They were business partners and neighbours, no more. The sooner she stopped playing these silly games, the quicker the whole nonsensical idea would have slipped back into the realm of fantasy, where it belonged.

'Remember,' she lectured herself, 'we started to fight with the first words we ever said to each other, and we haven't stopped since.' Except, of course, as that treacherous little voice in the back of her mind kept telling her, on those unaccountable times when they had found themselves almost in bed together.

'And being sexually attracted doesn't mean two people are in love, either,' she announced, and jumped a foot when the telephone rang.

'Ross,' she said eagerly, and pounced on the phone. Maybe he was calling to check if she was home, and then he'd come back, and——

'Kelly?'

'Oh. Hello, Maria.'

If Maria Clayton recognised the disappointment in Kelly's voice, she was too well-mannered to show it. 'Is Ross there, dear?'

'I'm sorry, he's gone out for the evening.' Why, she wondered, couldn't Allen's mother have been as nice as Maria Clayton was? If anyone had reason to be suspicious of her, it was Maria; after all, Kelly and Ross were practically living together. But Maria had never been impolite or nosy. Of course, Kelly reminded herself, Maria was just an ordinary human being. Mrs Parrish, on the other hand, considered herself a Leader of Society.

'Do you know if he's talked to Whitney today?'
Maria sounded preoccupied, as if she was troubled.

'I haven't any idea. I've been gone myself, you see.'
Darn you, Ross, she thought again. You could at least
have left a note!

'Well, I won't trouble him with it tonight,' Maria said,
as if she'd suddenly made up her mind about something.
'I'll call again in the morning. How are you, Kelly?'

In love with your son. For an instant, Kelly was
almost afraid she'd said it. 'The bookstore business has
been very slow for the last few days. I'm afraid Ross is
getting bored.'

There was a laugh in Maria's voice. 'I shouldn't
worry about it,' she said. 'Ross doesn't give up easily on
anything.'

Especially things like Whitney, Kelly told herself
hollowly. What was the problem that Maria had called
about? Quite obviously it involved Whitney. Was she in
some sort of trouble?

'Sometimes that tenacity is quite the most irritating
thing about him,' Maria added. 'Do tell him I'll call in
the morning, please.'

'Of course, Maria.' She put the phone down, and sat
there for a few minutes, looking at it thoughtfully.
Rapunzel climbed into her lap and started to purr.

Was Maria tired of the way Ross kept dangling after
Whitney? she wondered. After all, the woman might
want him to settle down, marry, have children so that
she could be a grandmother.

'Oh, stop it,' she told herself crossly. She didn't know
enough about any of them, really, to make any
judgements. Especially not Ross. The smartest thing she
could do would be to go to bed, cry herself to sleep, and
wake up in the morning with a new outlook . . .

Ross's key clicked in the door of his apartment. Kelly
heard it, and was hovering in the connecting door when
he came in and kicked the door shut.

Her hands were braced on the door frame, and she

had no way of knowing that the light from her own living room formed a sort of halo around her.

'Well, hello,' he said softly. He sounded just a bit as if the breath had been knocked from him. He set a big basket, piled high with clean clothes, on the counter beside the kitchen sink, and a flat box on the table. 'You're home early.'

'Not really.' Tears started to well in her eyes. 'Oh, Ross,' she wailed, 'where have you been?'

He raised an eyebrow. 'Doing my laundry and picking up a pizza. What does it look like?'

'But you didn't leave a note!'

'I expected to be home before the triumphant heroine——' He stopped short. 'And why I'm explaining it to you is beyond me. I am an adult, after all. Want a slice of pizza?'

'I'll eat anything that isn't French.'

He smiled at the distaste in her voice. 'It didn't go too well, hmmm?'

The gentle tone only made the tears come faster. But it wasn't Allen and her broken engagement that was making her cry, she knew. It was the knowledge that her flash of realisation had been correct, and that she loved Ross after all. It hadn't been her imagination, playing tricks on her. In the last few weeks, she had come to depend on his vitality, his strength, his intelligence. If those things were to be removed from her life now, she didn't know where she would turn.

He put the box on the coffee table in her living room, handed her a paper napkin, and settled back with a wedge of pizza and a satisfied sigh.

Kelly eyed him; he looked so much at ease in open-necked shirt, jeans, and boots. She wiped tears off her cheeks with the back of her hand and said owlishly, 'Mrs Parrish told me tonight that you were a shady character.'

He threw back his head and laughed. 'From her, that's as good as a reference,' he said finally.

He had a beautiful laugh, she thought, and realised
that in the whole evening she had spent with the
Parrishes, no one had laughed. In those endlessly long
hours, no one had made a joke, or seen a bit of humour
in anything that happened.

I couldn't stand to live in a house without laughter,
she thought, and was grateful once more that Ross had
brought her to her senses before she made the mistake
of marrying Allen.

Whitney is crazy, she thought, to have let this man
go. He was right about her husband, he was right about
Allen. The woman was nuts to let this prize get away.

But then, she reminded herself, Ross hadn't gone
very far. And whenever Whitney came to her senses,
he'd be right there, waiting.

He probably only cares about my problems, she
thought humbly, because it's a repetition of what
happened with Whitney—a girl making a foolish
mistake. But now that I'm not making that mistake any
more, and I realise how much I care about him——

The tears started to slide down her cheeks again.

Ross stretched an arm out across the back of the couch,
and said comfortably, 'Tell Uncle Ross all about it.'

The sympathetic tone only made her cry harder. She
buried her face in his shoulder and sobbed.

He sighed, and put his arms around her. 'If you don't
stop this,' he warned, 'Joe Keswick is going to think the
water pipes broke and flooded the whole building.'

She sniffed once.

'And the pizza's getting cold.'

'Is that all you care about?' she asked. She tried to
push away from him, but his arm tightened around her
like a steel band. 'Your blasted pizza?'

'It *is* my supper,' he pointed out. 'And if you insist on
soaking it, as well as me, with tears——'

'I can't help it if I'm upset,' she said, with dignity.
She blew her nose on the paper napkin and put her
head back on his shoulder. He was right. It was damp.

Ross sighed and handed her his clean handkerchief. 'Why do you keep tearing yourself up over this guy?' he said finally. 'He isn't worth it.'

'I know,' she said. 'That's why I told Allen tonight that I won't be seeing him any more. I'm not a complete dunce.'

'That statement is the first evidence I've seen of it,' he murmured.

'You,' she said icily, 'are the most irritating, annoying, irksome man I have ever met——'

'Without a doubt, you're right.' He looked down into her big blue eyes, and said huskily, 'Oh, hell, Kelly Green.'

He kissed her, harshly, fiercely. She gasped under the onslaught, and caught her breath. Her first instinct was to break away from him. Then she stared up at him through narrowed eyes. There's no reason on earth, she thought, why I should have to wait for Whitney to make up her mind! I'm going after what I want, and Whitney Lattimer will just have to look out for herself.

She stopped fighting and let herself be drawn even closer, till it seemed there wasn't room between them for a breath. But that was all right, Kelly thought, for she had apparently forgotten how to breathe anyway——

Her muscles seemed to have melted, too, she thought absently, and realised how wrong she had been to think that kissing Ross was merely exciting, when it was actually more like being on an out-of-control carnival ride, where frenzy and spine-tingling panic combined to send her blood pressure to feverish heights——

His hand had slipped up to cup her breast, and his thumb toyed with the shadowed triangle where the neckline of her dress ended. She had never known how sensitive her skin could be, but the gentle pressure of his hand was sending waves of ecstasy through her, as though she were a piece of driftwood being pounded against a rocky shore.

'Look,' Ross said, his voice uneven and hoarse, 'we're either going to have to break this up or go to bed.' His fingers slid reluctantly away from her breast, and he started to stand up.

'Fine.' Kelly clung to him, scrambling to her knees on the couch, and caught his hand, pulling it back against her warm skin. 'Let's go to bed.'

He was silent for an instant, then he laughed, without humour. 'I thought I saw danger flags flying in your eyes,' he mused. 'Look, Kelly Green, this is not a joking matter. You can't keep doing this to me and then backing out——'

'But I'm not backing out,' she pointed out breathlessly. She started to slowly unbutton his shirt, and let her hands slide under the smooth fabric to caress his chest. 'Don't leave me, Ross. Please——'

'Are you sure you're not just getting even with Allen?'

'I'm the one who told him to get lost, Ross, not the other way round.' Her fingertips were drawing intricate patterns on his skin.

'You're suffering from reaction, Kelly.'

She noted, with interest, that his voice was unsteady. How much like him it was, she thought. He had teased her, kissed her, tormented and caressed her, but he was too much of a gentleman to take advantage of her. He wanted to be certain this was her decision, and unless she was sure, he would wait.

'Quit it, Kelly,' he ordered. 'You're a pretty girl, and when you throw yourself at a man like this, only a saint could walk away.'

She smiled up at him and shook her head. 'I'm not asking for promises,' she whispered, and I don't want a saint. I want you.' My darling, she thought, I'm wise enough to know there are no guarantees in the game of love. All I want is a fighting chance to make you forget Whitney. She leaned forward, pressing her breasts against him, and kissed him, very slowly.

Somewhere in the middle of that kiss, they reached

the point of no return. He picked her up and carried her into her bedroom. Kelly was shivering with anticipation, and just a tiny thread of fear, as she fumbled with the rest of his shirt buttons. His fingers found the zipper at the back of her dress, and the tiny current of cool air touching her spine was like ice.

He undressed her gently, as if she had been a doll. His belt buckle seemed to jam under her touch, and she uttered a frustrated little moan.

He said with a breathless little laugh, 'I only hope this lives up to your expectations, Kelly Green,' and released the buckle himself.

She returned each caress with abandon, her body more truthful than even her thoughts could be about how much she wanted him, needed him. She pulled him down on to the bed, eager to be in his arms again without the artificial barriers that had frustrated her so.

But he would not be hurried. He made her wait as he stroked her skin and caressed her with his mouth, until she was half-mad with desire for him. Only then did he take her, gently at first, and then with a rising tide of vehemence that left her screaming his name when they reached the ultimate release.

It wasn't until the storm was over, and she lay quiet in his arms, his breath warm against her cheek, that she realised how much rigid control he had exercised, and how much power she had over him. She would have exulted in it, she thought vaguely, if she had only had enough energy left to care . . .

'No,' she said.

He raised his head and looked at her enquiringly. 'No, what?' he asked.

'That didn't meet my expectations,' she said breathlessly. 'That was so far beyond anything I ever dreamed of——'

He silenced her with a hard kiss, and then propped the pillows up against the headboard and pulled her up beside him with her head against his shoulder.

Kelly reached for the sheet, but he caught her hand. 'It's a little late for modesty,' he said. 'Let me look at you.'

'Modesty, nothing,' she said. 'I'm cold.'

He chuckled. 'I know a great cure for that,' he said softly, and teased the pink tip of her breast with a gentle finger.

Kelly shivered.

'Perhaps later,' he said, and tucked a blanket around her. She snuggled against him, drawing warmth from his body, and idly twirled his chest hair into little curls with the tip of her finger.

They didn't talk, but it was a comfortable silence. There was no need for words, she thought. What could mere words say, compared to the things they had told each other with their bodies?

A long time later, Ross sighed and said, very quietly, 'There's something I must tell you, Kelly Green.'

She mumbled something incoherent.

He glanced down at her closed eyes, at her hand lying lax across his chest. Then he smiled wryly and shook his head. 'Sleep well, my dear,' he whispered, and settled her against her pillow so she would rest more comfortably.

She murmured, and frowned, and then relaxed again. And while she slept, Ross, practical as always, wrapped himself in a blanket and went back to the living room to finish his pizza.

Her first drowsy thought as she awakened was a memory of Theodore Bear, the ragged, worn-out teddy bear that had slept with her till she was five and grew too old for stuffed animals in her bed. But Theodore Bear had never been so warm, or so large, and his ribs had been softly stuffed with cotton; they weren't hard and lean——

She opened her eyes. Her nose was buried against Ross's shoulder blade, and her breasts were pressing against his back. One arm was draped over him, and he was holding her hand against his chest.

Brazen, she thought. It must look as if you've been sleeping with him for years.

Then she remembered the details of the night before, and she smiled to herself. I've won, she thought. After what we have shared—he must care about me, or he wouldn't have held me like that, made love to me so tenderly. That was no one-night stand. He can't leave after that.

She leaned over him, her hair teasing against his shoulder. 'Wake up, sleepyhead,' she said softly.

His breathing was deep and even, but before she could say anything else he had rolled on to his back and pulled her down against him. 'You're a tease, Kelly Sheridan,' he announced, not bothering to open his eyes. 'And do you know what happens to teases?'

'No,' she said breathlessly.

His eyelids fluttered then. It was like looking down into the depths of a lake. 'This,' he said, his voice deep.

His arms locked around her so she couldn't move, and he pulled her head down till her lips met his in a long, warm kiss. 'And this,' he added, and suddenly she found herself pinned to the mattress by his weight, with his hands teasing sensuously over delicate skin that remembered for itself the madness of the night before.

Kelly tried to keep her voice even. 'Do you suppose we could just put a CLOSED sign in the bookstore window?' she whispered.

He grunted an answer. He was paying more attention to the little hollow at the base of her throat than to her words.

Then the telephone rang.

'Ignore it,' Kelly pleaded, but after the sixth ring even she couldn't put the insistent shrill out of her mind.

Ross swore softly. His hands lingered against her satin skin and then, regretfully, he pulled himself away. She shivered in the sudden cold, and reached for a blanket. But it was more than cool air that was making her shiver. There seemed to be a chill of fear settling round her heart.

He had left the bedroom door open, and she heard his brusque 'Hello.' Then there was a long silence.

Kelly huddled the blanket around her shoulders. It's all right, she told herself. In a minute, he'll put the phone down and come back, and everything will be just as it was . . .

Then she heard his voice, raised in irritation. 'Damn it, Whitney, this is not the time for this——'

Kelly stopped breathing. This is it, she thought. Now I'll know just what last night meant to him.

'Do you really need me?' he asked. It was quieter, no longer angry.

Another silence, but Kelly knew. Whitney will always need him, she thought, and he will always go.

She slid out of bed and reached for her long robe. She was determined not to be found waiting for him, expecting anything from him. She would not show him how deep this wound had gone, she told herself firmly. It was only her own foolishness that had caused it, anyway. He had made no promises, and she had known all about Whitney. She didn't even have the inadequate excuse of ignorance to justify her behaviour.

'All right,' Ross said. His voice was resigned. 'I'll leave right now, so I can be there this afternoon.'

She was making the bed when he came back. She didn't look up. Her hands were shaking as she straightened the blankets.

'I have to go into Chicago today,' he said quietly. He picked up the clothes he had discarded so casually the night before.

She nodded. She still wouldn't look at him.

'Don't look so glum,' he said. 'I'll be back by the end of the week.'

He has good intentions, she thought. But if Whitney needs him, everything here will be forgotten. The bookstore, the work still to be done ... And me, she added. If Whitney has decided that she wants him, he won't have a thought left for me.

When she didn't answer, he had quietly gone back to his own apartment. It was only minutes before he returned.

He was casually dressed, but he seemed to have put on a different personality. Gone was the leisurely, matter-of-fact Ross she had become to used to in the last few weeks, the one who was never in a hurry. In his place was a brisk, no-nonsense man. This was the one she had seen that first day, in Roger Bradford's law office—ambitious, driving, unable to sit still. The vacation is over, she told herself drearily.

He's on his way back to Whitney; of course he's in a hurry. She's finally called for him. He's thinking that perhaps she's changed her mind——

'Kelly Green,' he said, with a rough note in his voice. He turned her face up to his. 'You haven't said a word——'

She shook her head, and tried to suppress tears. What was there to say, after all? She was too proud to beg, and she knew in any case that begging would not stop him from going to Whitney. Nothing could stop him now.

'Goodbye, Ross.' She choked on the words.

He bent his head slowly, and kissed her lightly. But his thoughts, she knew, were already on the day ahead, not on her. The power she had felt in herself the night before was gone.

His hand lingered on her chin, and he said, thoughtfully, 'Maybe it's just as well. It will give us both a chance to think about what happened last night—what we want to do.'

She tried to smile, to pass it off as the joke it was. But her heart rebelled. You don't need to lie to me, she thought. I know the rules. I played the game, and I lost. It was sheer bad luck that Whitney chose today to get herself into trouble.

He glanced at his watch. 'I must go,' he said. 'It's a seven-hour drive.'

'You're not taking any extra clothes?' she asked slowly. Suddenly hope reawakened in her heart. If he was leaving all of his possessions behind——

'I don't want to take the time,' he said. 'I left some things at the apartment, anyway. I'll get by.'

Whitney's apartment? Jealousy stabbed through her like a javelin. Tonight he would be with Whitney. Dinner at their favourite restaurant, no doubt, and the rest of the evening at a night club. And then they would go back to Whitney's apartment, and open a bottle of champagne, and——

Kelly's head hurt at the idea.

He kissed her again, and said goodbye. He sounded almost apologetic, and it made her angry. At least he could be honest about how he felt, she thought. His eagerness to get away, to be back with Whitney, was almost like a scent in the room.

'Drive carefully,' she said, and stood there silent in the centre of her living-room until he was gone. Then she picked up a coffee mug and deliberately threw it as hard as she could at the wall.

Childish, she told herself, looking down at the broken china and regretting that she had lost control. She picked up each sliver of china as if she was doing penance for her temper tantrum, and then set about cleaning the whole apartment. Soon enough, it would be time to go downstairs for a whole day in the bookstore, a day that would allow far too much time to think. At least for the moment she could keep herself too busy to think.

The kittens roused when she moved the magazine basket, and Kelly allowed herself a few minutes to play with them. They were so tiny, but already they were showing signs of overpowering personalities. The little black one was the complainer, the leader in protesting whenever Rapunzel left the nest. He yowled sleepily when Kelly picked him up, and then settled down into the palm of her hand, purring throatily. 'You are a loudmouth,' she accused him lightly. 'You always have something to say, and you're never pleased with the way things are, while your little sister here only squeaks when there's something seriously wrong, and it takes a genius to get her to purr. Motormouth and Wordsworth—that's what I'll name you.'

She put the kittens gently back into the basket; Motormouth protested loudly. How easy life would be, Kelly thought, if she only had to deal with cats, and not complicated human beings who didn't have the sense to know when they were being used.

What was Whitney up to this time? she wondered. It seemed obvious to Kelly that the girl was a troublemaker. She might even have manufactured this problem simply to get Ross back to Chicago. She might have been afraid that if he was left alone too long with Kelly that something of the sort might happen——

'She might even be afraid of me,' Kelly decided, but then her bravado collapsed. What was there to be afraid of? Whitney Lattimer had crooked her little finger, and Ross had run, in such a hurry to be at her side that he hadn't even packed a change of clothes.

Kelly put the kittens' basket up in the windowseat, where it would catch the sun, and went downstairs to face the long day in the bookstore.

It was a slow day. No slower, of course, than many before had been, but then there had been Ross to talk to, to argue with, to entertain her with his dry sense of humour. Today it was just silent. Not even Joe Keswick showed up to try her patience, and the morning coffee crowd drifted down the street to watch an auction instead of hanging about for the usual chequers. Kelly felt deserted.

She was in the stockroom about midafternoon when she heard the bell jangle above the front door. She tried to put a pleasant expression on her face; this might,

after all, be an important customer. And heaven knew
she needed one today.

But she couldn't help showing some disappointmen
when she came into the store and saw the slicked-back
hair of the man checking out the titles on the bargain
table.

'May I help you, Mr Olsen?' she asked curtly.

He looked up with an oily smile. 'I think tha
depends, Kelly,' he said cheerfully, and came across the
store.

Kelly stepped behind the counter, putting it between
them as a barricade.

Olsen leaned on the glass beside the cash register and
said, 'Where's your partner today?'

Kelly's hands clenched in the pockets of her jeans
'He's stepped out for a moment,' she said finally.

He smiled. 'Well, that's all right. It's obvious to me
that you're the boss, despite all the partnership talk. So
why don't you and I get down to details. What do you
want, little miss?'

'For you to go away and stop trying to buy me out,
she said. 'Is that plain enough?'

Olsen laughed. 'But I'm not going to do that,' he said
softly. 'So let's talk money. Will five thousand make
you think about selling me all of Patrick's old stock?'

She stared at him for a long time. 'Why do you want
those old books so badly?' she asked finally.

'Call it sentiment. I was fond of Patrick.'

'And you were even fonder of the days when he
didn't bother to open the Bookworm half the time
which left you with a monopoly here in town,' Kelly
murmured.

He smiled. 'Call it that if you like,' he said. 'I'm
agreeable. Five thousand, and it's a deal.' He pulled a
cheque-book out of his hip pocket and flipped it open.

'If I was interested, Olsen, I'd want cash,' Kelly
pointed out.

He made a clicking noise with his tongue. 'You have

o trust people to do business,' he pointed out. 'But that
ould be arranged.'

'Except that I'm not interested,' she finished. 'Once
.nd for all, I am not going to sell this place. Now get
•ut!'

'But I'm not asking you to sell the store,' he objected
nildly, 'just the books.'

'It comes down to the same thing,' Kelly said.

'Think about it.' He turned toward the front door.
Any time you're ready to deal, Kelly, I'll be around.'

'That's what I'm afraid of,' she muttered.

But after he was gone, she kept thinking about it. It
.ad been a long, dull day; the few sales she had made
vouldn't pay for the electric bill, much less the rent and
.he interest on that bank loan.

How much of the pleasure had been the Bookworm,
.nd how much had been in being able to frustrate Ross?
he asked herself. Had she been so happy these last few
veeks, despite the worries of a new business, because of
.he bookstore or because Ross had been beside her?

Chastened, she had to admit that it was Ross. It
.idn't do much for her ego.

But there was no backing out now. She had to make
. go of it, or she couldn't pay back that loan. She
ouldn't make money selling musty old books——

And Olsen couldn't, either. So why did Olsen want
hem so badly?

'To drive me out of the store,' she murmured. But
losing the store had always been incidental to him, she
ealised. While he would like nothing better than to see
he Bookworm closed, he had never really tried to buy
he business—only the old books.

She stood in the middle of the store, in the gathering
;loom of evening, and looked around. What *was* it in
hese old books that Olsen wanted badly enough to pay
ive thousand dollars for them? He hadn't even looked
.round the store today, at the thousands of feet of
helving. He had glanced only at the bargain table——

She checked every book on the table. She inspecte[d] the bindings, the end papers, the copyright dates. The[n] she shook each volume, hoping that something loos[e] would fall out.

When she sat down an hour later in frustration, th[e] obvious hit her. If there had been something on th[e] bargain table that Olsen wanted, he would have simpl[y] bought it. It left her right back where she had been—thwarted, and feeling as if Olsen had looked at th[e] bargain table simply to kill a little time.

But if he had offered so much money, he must b[e] sure that what he wanted was still here.

'He didn't check the shelves,' she reminded herself[,] 'so he's certain it isn't there. It must be something tha[t] we would recognise if we saw it. That's why he hasn'[t] mentioned anything specific. He's offered to buy th[e] whole batch because he's hoping to sneak whatever it i[s] out of our hands before we even know we have it.'

She thought about it. It made a frightening kind o[f] sense.

'It must still be upstairs,' she said in dawning wonder[.] 'There is something in one of the books upstairs that i[s] valuable to Olsen. And it isn't just sentimental value, o[r] he would have told us what it was, and offered to bu[y] that one book.'

She looked around the store. Then she hung th[e] *Closed* sign in the window, turned off the lights, an[d] climbed the spiral stairs.

'A book that's worth five thousand dollars to Olsen,['] she mused. As she stood in the doorway of he[r] apartment, looking at the boxes of books that still line[d] the walls, she whispered, 'I wonder, I wonder——'

CHAPTER ELEVEN

SHE had no idea what she was looking for, and that didn't make the search any easier. It might be the book itself that was precious to Olsen; it might be a document concealed inside. It might be a rare bookplate, or an autograph, or a souvenir of some eccentric collector. It might be anything at all. But I have to look, she told herself firmly. I have to try.

The one sure thing was that Olsen knew what he was looking for, and once he had access to the books, it wouldn't take him long to find it. Now if she could only read his mind, Kelly thought. What was Olsen interested in? What were his hobbies, his amusements?

'Besides making passes at his salesgirls,' Kelly told herself drily.

But that line of thought was hopeless. She didn't know enough about the man even to speculate about his interests. And who wanted to think about Olsen, anyway? she asked herself. It was enough trouble to have to look at him now and then! She put the idea aside and opened another box of books.

Volumes were piled high around her by then. She checked each book carefully, flipping through the pages, looking at the title page, the publication information, the author. She inspected each binding to be certain nothing had been slipped down inside the spine, and entertained herself by speculating on what precious document Olsen might be looking for.

'A love letter he wrote to an old flame,' Kelly decided. 'But Patrick also loved the girl. So when she died of a broken heart after Olsen jilted her, she gave Patrick the letter, and he hid it here, so that if he ever needed to prove what a rotter Olsen was——'

Nice story, she decided, but unlikely. It was a little too much to swallow, the idea that Olsen could have ingratiated himself enough with any woman to have broken her heart!

'A will,' she decided next. 'Olsen's father had written another will, a later one that disinherited him. Then he died, and Olsen hid the second will so he'd get all of his father's money. But he mistakenly sold the book that he'd hidden it in to Patrick, and he's been trying in vain for years to get it back——'

It would have to be a mighty thin will to fit inside the spine of a book, she decided. But then, it didn't have to be in the spine. Some of these books had inserts and maps and other elaborate additions. It could be anywhere.

'Maps!' she exclaimed. 'A treasure map. There had been rumours for years about Jesse James and his gang hiding the loot from their bank robberies around here. Maybe the James Brothers drew a map, after all. All these years it was tucked away in someone's library, and after Patrick bought the books from the estate, the heirs realised what they'd sold. So they told Olsen about it, and——'

Why wouldn't they have come and told Patrick, and got the map back? she asked herself. Too bad that the solution to this treasure hunt of hers had to make logical sense!

'You're getting crazy from lack of food,' Kelly told herself. She dusted off her hands, climbed over the wall of books, and poked around in the refrigerator. Her bounty extended only to half a head of lettuce and the wild rice left over from the Cornish hens she had cooked for Allen's birthday. It seemed like a million years ago, she thought, since she had assumed herself in love with him, ready to marry him, wanting to do everything for him.

And now there was Ross. Or rather, there wasn't Ross, she reminded herself as she cut up the lettuce for a salad. She would be nothing more than foolish if she allowed herself to believe that he would be coming back.

She poked through his refrigerator and found a tomato and a slice of ham for her salad. She might as well clean out the whole thing, she decided. Who knew when he would remember it; by then everything would be spoiled.

She moved the basket of clean clothes into his bedroom and hung the shirts in the wardrobe. She felt a little guilty in even touching his things, as though he might resent it. But she couldn't keep herself from brushing a hand down the soft wool sleeve of one of his jackets and across the silky tailor's label with his name and the Tyler-Royale emblem on it. Then, as if the wool had burned her, she jerked away and closed the wardrobe door.

How immature, she thought, to have allowed herself to believe that because a man slept with a woman it meant that he cared about her! She'd chosen a hard way to learn the lesson, too. She was in love, all right— hopelessly, helplessly in love. There would never be another man who could be as all-important to her as Ross was, and last night's happiness would become a haunting memory as the years went by. Perhaps it would have been easier, she thought, if she didn't have that memory. She almost wished that she had been a wiser woman last night——

'Almost,' she said wryly.

She ate her salad, but it didn't taste very good, seasoned as it was with regrets and sadness. And then she went back to work.

By midnight she had gone through every book in her living-room and had started on the stacks and bookcases in Ross's apartment. He had never even looked at the books, she thought; he had just shoved aside those that had got in his way.

That fact alone should have told her Ross's opinion

of the bookstore. By now, if he'd had any intention of staying here, he would have shown some concern about his surroundings. But Ross had not cared.

And don't get upset about that, she lectured herself. Of course Ross hadn't refurnished his apartment. He had never pretended that his residence above the bookstore was anything but temporary. She had been an idiot to let herself believe that she was enough of a magnet to keep him in this little town, in this little store——

'Kelly,' she told herself firmly, 'you're a darn fool.'

She plunged into the stacks of books with more stubbornness than enthusiasm. Some of them were foreign editions, and she couldn't even read the titles. Many of the books were classics in elegant leather covers, but by this time an embossed binding was enough to bring a yawn to Kelly. She opened the glass doors of a sagging little bookcase in the corner, and emptied its contents on the floor.

The bottom shelf was full of Patrick's scrapbooks, and she rewarded herself for hours of labour by glancing through one of them. He had been a methodical old man, she decided. Every scrap of paper, every mention of the Bookworm in the local paper, had been saved. And pictures, here and there, snapshots and letters——

A faded photograph caught her eye. Written along the bottom of it, in a feminine hand, was, 'Ross and Whitney at the Mardi Gras ball. They call them the Inseparables. Whitney's husband is off to the left.'

Who would have sent Patrick such a picture, she wondered. Maria?

Kelly studied the photograph. It was unmistakably Ross, though a much younger one. Beside him, looking up at him, Whitney looked blazingly happy. The Inseparables, were they?—even with Whitney's husband in the room. Interesting, Kelly thought, and tipped the photograph so she could get a better look at Mr Lattimer.

He was portrait-handsome, but his Greek-god beauty was marred by the sulky, disgruntled twist of his mouth. Was it there because the couple nearby had conveniently forgotten all about him? Ross's arm was round Whitney; she was smiling. The neglected husband might have been miles away.

Kelly closed the scrapbook, thoughtfully. Which had come first, she wondered: had Whitney turned to Ross because she was unhappily married, or had her marriage collapsed because she was paying more attention to Ross than to her husband?

And in any case, what difference could it make to Kelly Sheridan? she asked herself. None, of course, so she should just go back to work.

She looked at Fenimore Cooper, at Blackstone's law commentaries, at Mark Twain, at Lewis Carroll, till her head was swimming and her eyes hurt. And she could find nothing that might prompt Olsen to pay five thousand dollars for the privilege of hauling these books away.

'This is ridiculous,' she told herself finally. 'The family Bible had a little value, so Patrick put it carefully in a box. Anything else that was important would be boxed, too.' She thought about it for a minute. 'Unless—is it possible that even Patrick didn't know that this mysterious thing had value?'

But then how could Olsen be so certain that Patrick had still owned whatever it was that he wanted so badly? Patrick could have sold it—'Whatever it is,' Kelly told herself hopelessly—any time in the last five years . . .

'Go to bed,' she ordered herself. 'You're not making sense any more.'

But her eyes refused to stay closed, even in the darkness of the bedroom. She could see books by the millions, stacked up around her, imprisoning her. The archaeologists might find her in this apartment a thousand years from now, as they had found the

victims of the volcano at Pompeii. She could see it now,
her skeleton buried and trapped by piles and piles of
books——

Suddenly she was falling, sliding down a dark tunnel
toward some unknown, terrifying destination. She tried
to scream, but no sound would come out.

She woke with a jolt, and sat up straight. 'Like Alice
in Wonderland falling down the rabbit hole,' she said
crossly, and punched her pillow into a heap. 'And you
never even liked to read it.' She dropped back against
the pillow wearily.

Less than two minutes later she was sitting up again.
There had been something different about that copy of
Alice in Wonderland; she had been almost too tired to
notice . . .

It took fifteen minutes to find it; the red binding had
disappeared beneath a stack of volumes printed in a
language that looked like Russian. She sat crosslegged
on the floor with *Alice* in her lap for a long time, afraid
to open it.

It was old. But was it old enough to be valuable?

She turned the book over and over. She had said,
herself, this afternoon, that when she discovered which
book it was that Olsen wanted, that she would
immediately recognise it, and know why he had wanted
it. But there seemed to be nothing special about *Alice*,
just this feeling, the nagging little something that tugged
at the back of her brain.

'You've short-circuited from lack of fresh air,' she
told herself abruptly. 'Endless hours of breathing the
aroma of old books, and it's no wonder you've gone
slightly bananas.'

She put *Alice* back in the bookcase, and went off to
bed. This time, only Rapunzel came to disturb her
sleep.

She wandered back and forth between the apartments
the next morning, munching on a slice of toast, hoping

that some inbuilt radar would guide her to Olsen's treasure. But the only thing that kept drawing her eye was *Alice*, lying in lonely state now in the glass-doored bookcase. Finally, she reached for the phone.

She had never talked to Oliver Amos, Ross's friend in the book department at Tyler-Royale, but if anyone could suggest a plan of attack, it would be him. She might end up looking like a fool for getting excited over a worthless book. He might even thoroughly embarrass her by mentioning her call to Ross, if Ross happened to stop in at the store while he was in the city.

'Fat chance of that,' she told herself. 'All his time will be tied up with Whitney.'

She waited in a rising state of panic while the Tyler-Royale switchboard put her call through.

'Rare books department,' said a clipped Eastern accent.

'I'm Kelly Sheridan,' she said. 'I'd like to speak to Mr Oliver Amos.'

'Yes? What may I help you with, Miss Sheridan?'

Kelly tightened her damp grip on the phone. This wasn't going to be easy, she thought. 'I believe you're a friend of Ross Clayton's?'

There was a brief silence. Then the voice, even more clipped, said, 'If there is something I can help you with, Miss——'

This isn't going well at all, she thought, panicky. She clutched the phone, and said, hurriedly, 'I believe he's talked to you about our bookstore—I'm his partner.'

'Yes.' Just the one word, still cool.

'I'm so sorry to bother you, Mr Amos, but Ross has been called away, and I have a book here that—well, I think it just might be valuable.'

There was the space of a breath. For a moment, Kelly was afraid that Oliver Amos had hung up on her. Then he said, with a perceptible trace of warmth, 'I see. And what is this rare book?'

She sighed in relief, and then, hurrying in case he

changed his mind, she read off all the information she could find on *Alice*'s cover and title page.

There was a long silence. 'Is it a red cloth cover?' he asked, when she had finished.

'Yes. How did you know that?'

He didn't answer. She was quickly finding that Oliver Amos was not a man to be pushed into words. 'It's possible that you have a—well, let's call it an unusual book,' he said finally. 'Before I could make any appraisal of value, I'd have to see it. Could you bring it in, Miss Sheridan?'

She gasped. 'I'm not exactly down the street from your store, Mr Amos. And there would be no one to run the Bookworm if I were to leave——'

She could almost see his shrug. 'That's up to you, of course. Pardon me for sounding rude, Miss Sheridan, but since you're inexperienced in these matters, I can't rely on your assessment of the book. I'm afraid I'm unable to go any further without seeing the condition of the volume.'

He'd certainly diagnosed the value of the family Bible in a hurry, she thought. But then, of course, perhaps he trusted Ross's powers of observation more than hers.

She glanced at her watch, and then at the red cloth cover of *Alice*. It must be unusual, she thought, or he couldn't have known what colour the cover should be.

'I'll be there this afternoon,' she promised recklessly, and started to put the phone down.

'Miss Sheridan!' he called.

'Yes?'

'Ah—you said you found this in a bookcase?'

'Yes. Why?'

'If there were any other books nearby, you might bring them along.'

'Mr Amos, I'd have to rent a moving van.' There was a pregnant pause, and then Kelly sighed. 'I'll bring as many as I can carry.'

'Thank you, Miss Sheridan. Of course, you must remember that it's probably nothing at all.'

That's right, she told herself glumly after the line was
dead. It was probably all in her imagination, and this
trip would be a waste of time and money. Why hadn't
he just told Oliver Amos she'd mail the darned thing to
him?

Because she couldn't stand the suspense that long,
she admitted to herself. She was afraid to even let
herself think that *Alice* might be special. She started to
stack books, trying to decide what to take to Mr Amos.
This one was extremely old, that one had an especially
pretty binding, another included some gorgeous colour
plates——

Joe Keswick was rocking by the fireplace down in the
store, placidly smoking his pipe. He looked startled
when Kelly came down with a backpack and a duffel
bag and started to empty the contents of the cash-
drawer into her pockets.

'I'm going to close the store for a few days, Joe,' she
explained. 'I have to make a business trip.'

He grinned. 'And what should I tell your young man
when he comes back and finds the money gone?'

'He's not my young man,' Kelly said, steadily. 'And I
doubt he'll be back in the next couple of days.'

'By the way, Kelly——'

'Joe, I don't have time for a conversation, all right? I
have to catch this morning's train.' She stuffed the roll
of wrinkled bills deeper into the pocket of her jeans.

'I just wanted to tell you that I signed the papers
yesterday. The building has been sold.'

'Oh.' She sighed. So much for one dream—that she
might strike it rich and be able to buy the building. 'I'm
glad for you, Joe.'

'I'll keep an eye on the place while you're gone,' he
offered.

'Thanks, Joe.'

He shrugged. 'I'm used to it. Did it long enough for
Patrick, didn't I?'

She slung the heavy backpack full of books over her

shoulder with a wince, and picked up the duffel bag. I
was loaded with books too, except for one pocket when
she had tucked a change of underwear. She was awfull
glad she hadn't packed a suitcase, she decided. In an
case, she wouldn't need too many clothes; she'd b
coming back tomorrow, regardless of Oliver Amos'
verdict.

I hope something in here has some value, sh
thought, shifting the straps of the backpack to lesse
the discomfort. I don't want to haul all of these roun
trip.

It was a glum thought to take on board the train. I
the books didn't have at least enough value to pay fo
her trip, she would come back to a store without a dim
in the cash register.

It was a little silly to worry about that now, she tol
herself. But at least, it was keeping her mind off Ro
and Whitney.

She hadn't been in the city in years, and then it ha
been only a guided tour, with a group of kids on
school trip. To be alone in downtown Chicago, hearin
the roar of city traffic, feeling the cold that seeme
always to linger between the skyscrapers, where the su
never penetrated, was a taste of freedom she hadn't fe
in a long time. No one knew where she was. No on
cared what she did. She could dance down the sidewa
and no one would notice, or she could disappear and n
one would be concerned——

That was a less than pleasant thought, Kelly decide
She paid the cab-driver and hoisted the backpack an
duffel bag again, glad that she didn't have to carr
them much further. She stood on the sidewalk for
moment, looking up at the imposing wrought-iron fro
of Tyler-Royale's block-square anchor store, and the
she took a deep breath and pushed through th
revolving door.

· The book department was huge, bigger than an

single store she had ever seen. Rows of tables and counters and display racks showed off the brilliant jackets of every new book imaginable. In the centre of the huge room the racks had been pushed back, and a table set up. People, most of them the picture of high-fashion elegance, were milling about the table. Behind it was a tiny elderly lady, perched on a high stool and almost hidden by a wall of books, signing her name. The poster that hung above her head announced that for the convenience and enjoyment of Tyler-Royale customers, Miss Carol Phillips would be autographing copies of her new book until seven o'clock that evening ...

Carol Phillips. Kelly bit her lip. So much for her idea of a young, glamorous, sexy woman whom Ross had seduced ... Carol Phillips could have been his grandmother.

And you, Kelly Sheridan, she told herself, were a jealous witch even then. You couldn't stand the idea of Ross being with any other woman, but it hadn't yet occurred to you that it was because you wanted him for yourself!

Well, there would be the rest of her life to analyse her problems. She stopped a clerk and asked to see Oliver Amos.

Tyler-Royale trained its employees well, she told herself. The young man in the conservative grey suit did not betray by so much as the flicker of an eyelash his astonishment at being told that the travel-stained young woman with the battered duffel bag was interested in the rare book department.

Oliver Amos was older than she had expected. That shouldn't have surprised her, though, she thought. Ross had some decidedly unusual friends ...

The white-haired old man rose, offered a hand, held her chair. He had the carriage of a much younger man, with square shoulders and an erect spine, and he wore a carefully tailored charcoal cutaway and striped trousers.

The elegant morning garb would have looked faintly ridiculous on anyone else, but it was the ideal Victorian setting for Oliver Amos.

There was a lively light of interest in his eyes as he settled himself behind his desk again, fingered his well-trimmed goatee, and said, 'May I see *Alice*, Miss Sheridan?'

Kelly unzipped the backpack. 'She's buried, I'm afraid. I thought she'd be safer packed in the middle.'

There was a split-second pause, and Kelly thought she could feel his disappointment. 'Very well. We'll take them in order.'

She started to pull out books and pile them on the desk. He picked one up, his long, elegant hands caressing the binding. 'Interesting,' he said. 'Junk, of course, but interesting. And this one—undisputed junk.'

Kelly's heart sank. 'They're of no value?' she asked.

'Oh—five to ten dollars, perhaps.' He was offhand about it.

'That's the sort of thing I've been selling for ten cents a pound,' Kelly admitted.

He looked up, an assessing light in his eyes. 'A unique approach, to say the least,' he murmured.

She pulled out a large volume. 'This is Chaucer,' she said. 'It's not very old, really, but it's so pretty that I thought——'

'Hmmm.' He ran a hand over the binding and opened the cover. 'This is one volume from a set of four,' he said, raising an aristocratic eyebrow accusingly.

'I didn't want to carry them all,' she pointed out.

'And the condition? Is this the best of them?'

'Actually, I brought it because it's the worst. I didn't think it would matter so much if I bent a corner on this one——'

'A folio reprint of the Canterbury Tales,' he murmured. 'Morocco backed boards, four volumes—— The set would be worth roughly a thousand dollars.'

Kelly's mouth dropped open. 'A thousand?' she whispered.

'Possibly more. I couldn't say till I've seen them all.' He set the Chaucer aside with a dismissive gesture. 'And old books are not exactly a liquid asset, you understand. I can sell it for you on consignment if you don't mind waiting for your money. You'll get a little more that way than I can offer you as a dealer.'

Kelly was still thinking about the Chaucer. She had hoped that some collector somewhere might pay a hundred dollars or so for it. But ten times that much——

And the *Alice*, Miss Sheridan?'

'Oh. I'd forgotten all about her.' She pulled the volume out. 'It's not much compared to the Chaucer set, I'm afraid.'

Indeed, the little red cloth book looked almost forlorn beside the big leather-bound Chaucer with its gold stamping. But Oliver Amos looked at it eagerly, from all sides, before he stretched out a careful hand to pick it up.

It was fifteen minutes later before he put *Alice* down, with a sigh, and tented his fingers together, looking at her over the tips of them. He seemed to be at a loss for words.

'Well,' Kelly said, 'I didn't expect it to be anything, of course. Did you want to buy the Chaucer?'

'Miss Sheridan, do you know anything at all about Lewis Carroll?'

Kelly shook her head. 'Very little. Why?'

'And yet you picked this book out of hundreds of others——'

'Thousands,' Kelly corrected. She could still see those stacks of books, whenever she closed her eyes.

'What drew you to this book?'

Who cared, she wondered. 'It was just a feeling,' she said. 'And it's obvious that——'

'Do you want a job, Miss Sheridan?'

She was speechless, confused by the sudden change of subject. 'What on earth do you mean?'

'You walked into a roomful of books and, without even recognising it, picked up a Tenniel *Alice*. There are collectors who would sell their souls, their grand-mothers, to own that book, Miss Sheridan.' He looked down at it, lying innocently on the blotter, and the glance was like a caress.

'What did you call it? A Tenniel *Alice*?' she asked, stumbling over the pronunciation.

'Yes. And in the best shape that I've ever seen.' He signed. 'You see, Miss Sheridan, I can teach you the facts about books—and obviously I'll have to. But you have the instinct. Not many people do, which is why my assistants don't last long around here.'

Kelly reached for the book. 'I still don't quite understand. Do your mean it actually is valuable?'

'Sir John Tenniel,' he instructed patiently, 'was a cartoonist and illustrator who made the pen-and-ink drawings for the 1865 edition of *Alice's Adventures in Wonderland*. It's extremely rare. One went at auction last year for twelve thousand dollars. But then,' he shrugged, 'it was not in as good a condition.'

Kelly sagged in her chair. 'I'll have to tell Ross right away,' she mused. 'I can't make any arrangements about selling it without him, of course. But I don't know where he is.'

'It should be no problem to find him. And about the matter of the job, Miss Sheridan?'

'Oh. Well, I'm quite flattered, but——' I couldn't bear to work for Tyler-Royale, she thought, and know that I might run into Ross without warning. But it was flattering, she thought. She had liked this old man on sight, and she was quickly developing a healthy respect for him. To work with rare books, old books——

No. Even if Ross travelled most of the time, it would still be too much to bear, to know that he was here sometimes, with Whitney . . .

'Perhaps it's a little early for that,' Oliver Amos conceded. 'I think perhaps I should make a trip out to your store to see the rest of these books. If we have a Chaucer folio and a Tenniel *Alice*, who knows what might be in the attic?'

I wonder what treasures I've already sold, she wondered. Or what might still be there. No wonder Olsen wanted those books! For five thousand dollars, he'd have been stealing them. But with the proceeds from the old books she could pay off the bank loan, she could afford a larger inventory, she might even drive Olsen out of business! 'That sounds like a wonderful idea,' she agreed.

'Very well. I'll make the arrangements right away. I'm sorry to have kept you in suspense about the *Alice*, by the way, but there have been reproductions of that edition.'

'Oh, I quite understand.' She looked at the innocent volume on the blotter. It hardly seemed possible, she thought.

'In the meantime, would you like me to put *Alice* in the vault?'

'Oh, yes, please.' She relinquished the book with relief.

'I'll give you a receipt, of course.' He handed her a slip of paper. 'Oh, here is Mr Clayton now. I was sure that he'd be down to see Miss Phillips during her party.' He waved a hand towards the glass office wall, and said, with satisfaction, 'He saw me. He'll be here in a minute, Miss Sheridan.'

The note of respect in his voice startled her. She turned towards the main part of the store. There was Ross, beside Carol Phillips at the table. But it was a different Ross. Something was subtly changed about him. It wasn't just a matter of clothes, either, though he was dressed, like Oliver Amos, in formal morning clothes. It was something in the way he stood, as if he was used to having his orders obeyed . . .

'I travel for a chain of department stores,' he had said. But travelling salesmen didn't wear that sort of thing. The ordinary floor clerks were dressed in grey suits——

'Mr Amos,' she asked, and turned to look at him. 'Just what is Ross Clayton's job in this store?'

'His job?' The old man's voice quivered just a little. 'I'm not sure that——'

'If you don't tell me, Mr Amos, I'll go and ask one of your clerks,' she said politely.

'It's all right, Oliver.' The voice from the office door was like an icicle on Kelly's spine. 'Why did you follow me, Kelly?' he asked. 'I told you I'd come back and wind things up at the Bookworm. Didn't you believe me?'

She was stunned. 'I don't have to explain anything to you,' she said, low-voiced. 'But since I'm here, perhaps you'd like to answer my question, Ross?'

'My official title is chief executive officer,' he said finally.

'And your boss? What's her title?'

He hesitated, and then said quietly, 'My mother is chairman of the board.'

'I see,' she said, very softly. 'It must have amused you, to pretend for me. To play the part of an ordinary working guy. Some vacation you had this year!' She picked up her backpack and duffel bag, both empty now and light. 'But I don't call it pretending, Ross. I call it lying. It was all lies——' Her voice caught.

'I would have told you,' he said. 'I wanted to tell you——'

'Of course you did,' she said sweetly. 'It was just that you never found the right opportunity.' Her face hardened. 'Well, there were a million opportunities, Ross Clayton—and you blew every one of them.'

He stretched out a hand, and she shrugged it off. 'You win,' she said. 'We'll sell the store after all, because I don't want to have to answer to you ever gain. And then we'll be free, Ross, as if Patrick had ever made that foolish will and caused us both so much damned trouble . . .'

She was almost running as she left the book department. She knew that he called her name once, and she also knew that he didn't follow her. She lost herself in the crowd on the lower floors, and found her way out to the street despite the tears that threatened to blind her.

She had lost her bookstore, and her love. Right now, she didn't know which one she cried for. And she didn't care.

CHAPTER TWELVE

IT had taken Oliver Amos a full day to sweep throug the entire building, pulling books off shelves right an left, designating some to be shipped back to h department at Tyler-Royale, some to be sold on Kelly bargain table, and some to go straight to the dump.

She had followed him around the Bookworm all day having difficulty keeping up with the old man's pace and learned more about old books in that twelve hou than she had imagined there was to know. Then he ha gone back to Chicago, hand-carrying the most preciou of the treasures they had found, and she had spent th rest of the week packing up the remainder to b shipped.

For Patrick, it seemed, had been a quiet collector off-beat books. 'The Tenniel *Alice* is without questio the diamond of the collection,' Oliver Amos had said the close of his whirlwind tour, 'but there are som rubies and pearls and opals scattered about.'

'I wonder why he didn't list the books in his will Kelly murmured. She had been sitting at her kitche table, hands curled around a coffee mug, thinkin about how good a soak in a hot bath would feel to h aching muscles. 'We could have missed them so easily

Oliver Amos had smiled. 'He probably hoped tha the accountants, at least, would miss them,' he pointe out. 'If you tell your attorney, it's going to cost yo quite a bit of their value to settle the estate ta Officially you could list them as old books of negligib worth——'

But that would be dishonest, Kelly knew. And rig now, after the way Ross had treated her, anything tha hinted of dishonesty made her shiver. So, this mornin;

she was packing the last box of books and waiting for
Roger Bradford to return her phone call.

'There,' she said to herself, smoothing down the final
strip of packing tape. Her voice was loud in the empty
store. 'That's the last of them.'

Now that the last box was safely packed, she could
reopen the store and begin her going-out-of-business
sale. The signs were already in the window; all she had
to do was walk over to the door and turn the key. But
instead, Kelly sat on the edge of the counter nibbling on
a fingernail and thinking.

It had been a week since that day in the book
department at Tyler-Royale, when the little game of
deception that Ross had been playing for weeks had
become so blatantly clear. It still hurt whenever she
thought about it. 'He didn't have to lie to me,' she said
aloud.

She should have seen through it, she thought.
Travelling salesmen didn't drive sports cars like that one.
And though they might dress nicely, they usually didn't
wear hand-tailored jackets, either. She should have seen
from the beginning that Ross was a fraud——

And it wouldn't have made a bit of difference, she
told herself. You fell in love with him as he was, with
the charm and the brilliance and the sense of humour.
It had nothing to do with his job. You loved him as a
travelling salesman, and you still love him, despite the
fact that he lied to you. It wouldn't make any difference
to you if he dug ditches for a living; he's still Ross
Clayton.

But it might have mattered to Whitney, she thought.
Had Whitney threatened him—told him to give up the
silly little bookstore and get back to the real job, or lose
her? It was possible, Kelly conceded. And in a way, she
didn't blame the woman; it must have seemed to her
like a stupid prank.

But why couldn't Ross see that Whitney didn't care
about what made him happy?

'And what,' Kelly asked herself bluntly, 'makes you think that he was any happier here at the Bookworm than he was at Tyler-Royale?' He certainly hadn't seemed lost in gloom that day when she had seen him at the department store—at least until he'd spotted her. She put a hand to her flushed cheek. It wasn't going to be easy to put this thing behind her.

She slid off the counter and went to unlock the door. There was no point in putting it off any longer; the remaining stock had to be sold and the store closed, and there was no sense in waiting around for Ross to come back and give her his opinion. She hadn't heard from him in a week, and she wasn't going to hear from him now.

Roger Bradford was getting out of his car across the street. She waited in the doorway for him, turning her face up to the sunshine. Summer was fast approaching: she tried to tell herself that she would be glad not to be shut up in a bookstore during the prettiest season of the year.

'I didn't expect you to stop by,' she said as the attorney came in. 'I just needed to talk to you a minute.'

'I have something for you.' He had a long envelope in his hand. 'I've been carrying it around for a couple of days, trying to catch you. But the store's been closed.' There was a question in his voice.

'That's what I needed to talk to you about.' She led the way to the fireplace, offered him a chair, and handed him a list of the valuable books.

When she was finished with her story, Roger Bradford glanced through the inventory and said, with a delighted grin, 'So Patrick, the sly old fox, almost pulled one over on me. I wonder if that's what's in here?' He tapped the long envelope against the table, and then handed it to her.

Her name was on the front, in the wavering, spidery handwriting that she had learned to recognise. 'From Patrick?' she asked.

Roger Bradford nodded. 'He attached it to his will, and asked that I give it to you sixty days after he died. The time was up last weekend, but you've had the store closed. Are you going to sell out?'

She nodded.

'Well, I'm not surprised. I knew Ross had gone back to Chicago,' he said.

'I suppose the whole town knows it.' Then, curiously, 'Why didn't you ever tell me he was the boss at Tyler-Royale?'

'Do you know, Kelly, I think that's the only question you didn't ask me,' he said gently. He rocked quietly for a few moments, and then stood up. 'I'll leave you to your letter,' he said. 'I'd better get on to the office.'

The coffee crowd began to trickle in just then. They seemed to have a sixth sense that told them when the bookstore opened, she thought, for in less than fifteen minutes the whole crowd had assembled. They seemed subdued today, though, because the sign in the window meant that their gathering place would again be taken from them.

'The coffee's on me from now on, guys,' Kelly announced. 'And as long as I'm here, you're welcome to come in. I just don't know how long that will be.'

'And we were finally getting this end of town straightened out,' one of the men grumbled. 'Now that the developer has bought Joe's building and the rest of the block, you move out.'

Kelly was thinking about her early idea of a row of craft shops all along this gently-shaded street. Now that dream would come true, but it would be someone else's dream. But perhaps, if the books produced enough money, she could come back here with another kind of shop——

No, she told herself. You'd be a lot better off to get completely away from this little town, and make a fresh start somewhere else.

She remembered the envelope in her hand, and

retreated behind the counter to open it. What had
Patrick wanted to say to her that had to wait sixty days
after he was dead?

'Kelly Green,' the letter began, and suddenly it was
as if she could hear his voice again, tinged with the
slight brogue that crept in whenever he was feeling sad
or sentimental. 'By now two months have gone, and I'm
hoping you'll not remember me with sadness . . .'

When she put the letter down a few minutes later, she
was laughing at the silly, melodramatic, matchmaking
old fellow, and at the same time she was crying for
herself and for the dream that Patrick cherished.

'For I'm thinking, Kelly Green,' the old man had
written, 'that it will not take you sixty days to know
your mind. And if Ross is the man I think him, he'll
know too. 'Twould take a fool to overlook you, and
Ross is not a fool. And if perhaps I'm wrong, and
there's no love between you, then I'm begging your
pardon, Kelly Green . . .'

The old man had set them up, she thought, wiping
tears from her cheeks with the back of her hand. He
had purposely thrown them together in the hope they
would fall in love. It was frightening how accurate
Patrick had been; he might almost have read her mind.
But he hadn't taken Whitney Lattimer into account,
and so the Inseparables would remain together, and
Kelly Green would be alone.

Rapunzel leaped up on the counter and rubbed
against Kelly's arm. 'Except for you, Rapunzel,' she
said. 'I'll take you and Motormouth and Wordsworth
with me. Wherever we're going.'

The kittens were at her feet. She stooped and picked
up Motormouth, who protested and then settled down
into her arms with a blissful purr that sounded like a
chain-saw. The kittens' eyes had opened in the last
couple of days, and they were now ready to attack the
world.

'If I'd known,' she said, wincing as Wordsworth's

claws dug into her ankle, 'I'd have named one of you Lewis Carroll——'

The front door banged open, and she jumped and wheeled around to face a furious Ross. 'What in the bloody hell is the meaning of that sign?' he shouted, gesturing at the banner in the window.

'How very interesting. I always thought you could read standard English, Ross,' she retorted. 'It says we're liquidating. Selling out. Closing down. Going out of business——' She was thinking, he's here, he's come back—his tan has faded, but he's still frighteningly handsome . . . 'I told you we were through.'

'You can't close the store without my permission,' he announced.

'So sue me. Now that there's a little money involved, no doubt you'll find an attorney who would be delighted to take care of the legal end.'

'Kelly, dammit——' He reached for her.

She stepped away from him. 'No more of your little parlour tricks, Ross,' she warned. 'No more lessons in controlling my temper, or other forms of abuse. Don't touch me.' She saw, over his shoulder, that the chequers game had come to an abrupt halt. The members of the coffee crowd were craning their necks so they wouldn't miss a line of this more absorbing play.

'We have an audience,' she murmured.

'Do you think I give a damn who's watching?'

No, she thought. He was so angry right now that nothing would have stood in his way. Why? she wondered idly. After a week of silence, to be suddenly attacked like this was more than she could understand.

'Why are you here, Ross?' she asked quietly.

'I came to talk some sense into you, and to pick up my clothes.'

She turned away, and her hand clenched on Motormouth's fur. The kitten yowled, and Kelly bent to put him down.

I should have known it was nothing more personal

than that, she thought. All he wanted was his clothes, while she ached to be in his arms again—to have him close to her ... But I will not betray myself to him, she resolved. 'Too bad you didn't let me know you were coming,' she said lightly. 'I could have had everything packed and waiting on the doorstep.'

'That's exactly why I didn't call you,' he said. 'I wanted to see for myself what you were up to. But this——' He waved a hand at the window. 'Kelly, don't be a fool!'

'I thought you wanted the store closed.'

There was a pause. Then he said heavily, 'That was a long time ago.'

'So it was. And if you can change your mind, so can I.' She reached for the feather duster. 'I don't suppose you meant that you want to stay here and run the Bookworm?'

'Of course not. I have to go back to Chicago.'

'Then why should you care if I want to sell it?' she asked. She started to dust sleeves. 'You're plenty busy with Tyler-Royale; I should think you'd be relieved to get rid of this headache.'

He followed her across the store. 'Oliver said he offered you a job, and you turned him down. Why?'

'What does it matter to you?'

The coffee crowd, she saw, was avidly following the progress of the argument. All pretence of playing chequers was gone.

Ross said, 'I thought you didn't want to work for him because you wanted to keep this store open.'

'Wrong, Mr Clayton. I would love to work for Oliver Amos. Unfortunately, he wouldn't really be the boss—you would be. And frankly, after surviving a partnership with you, I wouldn't work for you if I was starving!'

His jaw tightened, and Kelly swallowed hard. It had been a dirty thing to say, she knew. And it hadn't been very wise——

But his next words were subdued. 'I should have told you about Tyler-Royale.'

'You certainly should have—Mr Chief Executive Officer!' Her voice was bitter.

'I admit that I was wrong about you. All those things I suspected of you and Patrick——'

The coffee crowd, in unison, uttered a strangled cough. Kelly glared at them. They looked embarrassed and shuffled back to the chequer board.

'You have to admit that it didn't look good—Patrick leaving everything he owned to a young, pretty girl like you——'

'Half of it,' she said sharply, 'remember? You got the other half.'

'Yes,' he admitted. 'And I wondered why, at the time. At any rate, I didn't want you to know about Tyler-Royale. I was afraid——'

'Of what?' She brandished the duster at him. 'That I'd try to get my claws into you as I had into Patrick? Damn you, Ross Clayton!'

'Something like that,' he said. 'And then, when I realised that you hadn't been after Patrick's money, it was too late to tell you. In any case, it didn't seem to matter—then.'

That much was right, she thought. What he was hadn't mattered. The fact that he hadn't told the truth about it—that was important.

'I want you to have the bookstore, Kelly. I'll be a silent partner, and let you run it as you choose. I'll even sell you my half-interest, if that's what you want, at whatever terms you want to make——'

'I don't want your charity!' She was almost screaming. 'And if you say you owe it to me for what happened the other night, I'll—I'll throw something at you!'

There was a long silence. 'Kelly.' His voice was soft. 'Was that night special for you, or was it just my imagination?'

She swallowed hard. 'Of course it was nothing special,' she said. Sarcasm dripped from every word. 'I make a habit of it. I'll go to bed with any man who'll share his pizza——' Her voice broke, and she leaned against the rank of shelves, trying to hide her face.

He put a gentle hand on her shoulder. 'Kelly Green——'

'Don't call me that!' she ordered, shaking his hand off. 'Don't touch me. You've hurt me—you've lied to me——'

There was a long silence. 'Kelly, I came back here to apologise,' he said. 'I didn't treat you well, and I'm sorry. I didn't intend to rip up at you today, either. I don't know what happens to me—I just can't stop myself from yelling at you.'

She nodded, miserably. She wouldn't look at him.

'Will you please take the bookstore? Patrick intended you to have it.'

'If that was what he wanted,' she whispered, 'he'd have left you out of the will.'

She could hear the smile in his voice. 'No, he wouldn't, the scheming old fox,' he said. The smile dried. 'It wasn't Patrick's fault that his grand plan didn't work out.'

Apparently Ross had received a letter, too. So that was why he was suddenly solicitous—because he was paying off a debt to his dead relative! Kelly couldn't look up at him; her control would have broken, and he would have seen the devastation in her eyes. She thought, I cannot bear it if he feels sorry for me . . .

'I don't want it,' she said. 'You're the one with the business head. I can't run it alone.'

'You know I can't stay here,' he said softly. 'I have a job to do at Tyler-Royale. I can't just walk out on it.'

'Of course I know. Whatever makes you think I want you to stay?' She sounded a little querulous, she knew.

'I mean it, you know, about you having the store. With the income you'll be getting from the rare books, you can get a head start.'

And with the new developer promoting this whole neighbourhood, she thought, it would be easier.

'But if you're positive you don't want it, Kelly, then we'll sell out together.'

She let the silence drag out. I can't, she thought. I can't bear to live here, work here, and remember him. 'I'm certain I don't want the store,' she said finally.

It's over, she thought. He'll go away, and I won't see him again.

'Then what will you do, Kelly?'

'I can't see that it's any of your business.'

'But you'll stay here?'

She shrugged. 'Probably.'

'If you're looking for a job—Oliver Amos wants to train you. He thinks you're a phenomenon.'

How much she would love to work with that elegant old man, to learn from him all he could teach . . . She shook her head. That would also mean that she might see Ross every day, or run into Whitney when she came to the store. And Whitney would look at her, and know that she loved Ross. The Whitneys of the world always knew . . .

'I don't want to move to Chicago,' she said. 'Look, Ross, you don't have to take care of me. You don't have to make a job for me. Or are you're worried about me paying off my debts?' she asked with a challenging look. 'I'll pay my half of the bank loan just as soon as *Alice* sells. I can trust you, can't I, to send me my share?'

He looked at her steadily for a long moment. 'You can trust me,' he said.

She dusted quietly for a while. He stood there, leaning against the shelves, watching her. Finally she looked up. 'Shouldn't you be upstairs packing?' she asked. She couldn't stand his watchful silence. He seemed tense, as if he was about to pounce.

'Probably.' But he didn't move. 'Are you so anxious to get rid of me, Kelly?'

Kelly shrugged. 'I just don't want you to get into more trouble with Whitney by hanging around here. I'm sure you told her that you wouldn't stay long.'

He smiled, ruefully. 'You're right, you know. And Whitney is livid that I came back at all. She seems to think you'll convince me to stay here.'

She was sorry she'd mentioned Whitney. It hurt just to listen to the way he said the woman's name—it was obvious from the tone of his voice how deeply he cared about her.

'Why would I want to keep you here?' she said sharply. 'Once I've got the money for the *Alice*, and the rest of these books are sold, Whitney will have nothing to worry about.'

There was wary interest in his eyes, and a long silence stretched out between them. She dusted another shelf, hardly seeing what she was doing.

He reached into his hip pocket and pulled out a cheque-book. 'It may be a while before *Alice* sells,' he said. 'I'll give you a few thousand in advance——'

'Keep your damned money,' she said, without heat. 'I told you I don't want your charity.' She moved on to the next rank of shelves. He followed her and propped a slip of paper between two books next to her hand.

'You'll need some cash,' he said.

'That doesn't mean it has to be your money.'

'It isn't a gift, Kelly. I'll keep it out of your share.'

'I'll survive without it.'

He shrugged. 'As you like.' But the cheque stayed there, defiant. She didn't look at it. He said, finally, 'Whitney thought at first that my coming out here was only a whim, you know.'

'I really don't care what Whitney thought.' She tried to say it coolly, with disdain. But it came out in a cracked mumble instead.

'Don't you?' he asked softly. 'It took quite a bit of explaining to talk her around.'

Kelly swallowed hard. 'Do you mean you told her all about it?' she whispered.

He seemed surprised. 'Of course. It's part of the new programme of honesty that you recommended.'

She was horrified. She turned away from him with a little shrug. 'And then she forgave you?'

'Oh, she's still slightly put out. I can't say that I blame her, but she'll get over it once I'm back in Chicago permanently.'

He was so matter-of-fact about it that it disgusted her. 'Of course,' she agreed coldly. 'You're very persuasive when it comes to these matters.'

'Do you think so?' He considered that one, turned it over in his mind, and then shook his head. 'No, I can't agree with you there. I'm doing so badly when it comes to the important things, you see.' His voice was husky.

But if he and Whitney had patched it up, what other important matters were there? Kelly was becoming confused.

'I was surprised when Patrick named me in his will,' Ross mused. 'I was never close to him. I thought at first he'd done it because he was suspicious of you, and he wanted someone to keep an eye on you. Then, by the time I realised what the old fox was really up to, it was too late. I couldn't just walk away from the Bookworm. But by then I'd lied to you——'

Kelly turned her back. 'I'm sorry if you suffered any embarrassment over Patrick's ideas,' she said stiffly. 'I certainly don't want you to feel that I expect anything from you, or that I had any idea what Patrick wanted. After all, I knew all about Whitney.'

'Did you?' he asked cryptically. His voice was soft. 'She'd like to meet you, Kelly-Green-with-envy——'

'Don't call me that!' She took a firm hold on her temper and went on quietly, 'You've made your choice, Ross. It was the only choice you could make, and I respect it.'

'And now you have to make yours. I know you don't

like Chicago, but come back with me anyway, Kelly
Once you've met Whitney, you'll understand why I
can't just leave her in the lurch——'

She exploded. 'No! Damn it, Ross, stop this! I can't
stand it any more! I won't share you with that—that
insufferable snob!'

'I won't tell her you called her that,' he said
comfortably.

She threw the duster at him. 'And I won't stay here
any longer and listen to how much you love her. I can't
bear to hear you! Go back to her if that's what you
want, but stop tormenting me, Ross!' Her eyes were full
of tears, burning and blinding. But she thought she saw,
through the fog, a smile come to his lips. It was a tender
smile, a tremulous smile——

You're imagining things, Kelly, she told herself
furiously.

'Don't forget to cash your cheque,' he said mildly,
and put it in her hand.

'All right, I will cash it, because I need the money, and
because you owe me something for all the trouble you've
put me to——' She glanced down at the slip of paper in
her hand and started to cry in earnest. 'Ross, you bloody
idiot, you can't even put the right name on a damned
cheque!' She crumpled it up and threw it at him.

Ross caught the paper ball and straightened it out. 'I
thought it was a good idea,' he mused, 'Kelly Clayton.
It has such a nice ring to it. But I guess you won't be
able to cash it till you marry me.'

Kelly turned on the bottom step, unable to believe
that she had heard him right. He was leaning against a
rank of shelves, his arms folded across his chest, the
cheque dangling negligently from his fingers. He looked
perfectly at ease.

The coffee crowd, all pretence long since gone, was
hanging over the backs of chairs and around the edges
of shelves, mouths open, in rapt attention.

'You had me fooled for a little while,' he said, a smile

tugging at the corner of his mouth, 'with all the talk about not wanting to live in the city, and about wanting to keep the bookstore. I tried to tell myself that I just wanted you to be happy, whatever it took, and that I'd ruined my chances when I didn't tell you the truth about my job. But it wasn't that, was it? Because you don't want the bookstore after all, and I don't think you're all that upset at the idea of moving——'

It was Whitney, she wanted to say. I knew I couldn't compete with her . . .

'And then you started talking about Whitney,' he murmured, as if he had read her mind. 'You've thought all this time that I wanted to marry Whitney—haven't you?'

She looked at the floor to avoid those unflinching blue eyes. 'You told me weeks ago that you loved her,' she whispered.

'I do. But don't you know there's a difference?' His voice was warm now, gentle. 'If you had only told me what you were thinking, Kelly Green——'

'How could I?' She bit her lip.

'When you started talking about Whitney today, you tried to be calm, but you couldn't hide how jealous you were of her. It wasn't until then that I realised what a fool I'd been.' He started slowly across the room towards her. 'It's a fact of life, you see, Kelly Green, that when you marry one twin, you have to take the other one as well.'

'Twins?' she whispered faintly.

'Incredible as it sounds, my love, you're jealous of my twin sister.' He smiled down at her. 'That glorious green streak just wouldn't stay hidden. And now I know that I matter to you. I think you love me just as much as I love you.'

'You and Whitney——'

'She's five minutes younger than I am, and she's spent the last thirty years trying to catch up,' he said. 'They called us The Inseparables——'

'I know,' she said weakly. The photograph of them—
they really were brother and sister? Whitney's cloud of
dark hair, those huge dark blue eyes—why had she
never seen the resemblance? Kelly's head was spinning.

'Would you like to see where we're listed in the
family Bible?' he asked finally. He was holding her by
then. It felt so incredibly right to be back in his arms,
and to know that this was for always.

It was right in front of me, she thought. If I had only
looked a little farther——

'Whitney's been a little jealous of you, too,' he added.
'And afraid that if you didn't want to live in Chicago,
she'd be stuck with Tyler-Royale.' His fingers were
winding through her hair. 'If you hate the city so
much,' he said softly, 'we'll find another way——'

'I'd live in an igloo,' she confessed. 'Anywhere, to be
with you.'

It was a long, warm, and satisfying kiss. At least it
would have been if it hadn't been interrupted by
applause from the coffee crowd. Ross sketched a bow
towards them and said politely, 'You can either go back
to chequers or you can leave, but my fiancée and I are
not going to provide the entertainment any longer.'

'You been doing a good job so far,' one of the
regulars chuckled unrepentantly.

Ross ignored him, and looked down at Kelly. There
was a light in his eyes that she had never seen before.
'You will marry me?' His voice was almost harsh.

A silky paw brushed her ankle. Kelly looked down at
Rapunzèl, and then up at Ross. 'What about the cats?'

'Must we take the cats?'

'Patrick trusted me to take care of them.'

He sighed. 'So he did. And he trusted me to take care
of you. Will you let me do that?'

His hands were gentle, sending shivers through
Kelly's body. She nodded. She couldn't talk just then.

The tension seemed to ooze out of him. 'I must
admit,' he mused, 'that it will be a lot tidier than the

lternative. If you were to refuse me, I'd have to sue
ou—as the co-executor of Patrick's will—for holding
ut on my inheritance . . .'

His voice was muffled a little, because he was
ibbling her earlobe. 'Because you, Kelly Sheridan,' he
dded huskily, 'are by far the most valuable part of
'Hara's Legacy.'

She closed her eyes and put her head down on his
noulder, feeling as if she had come home.

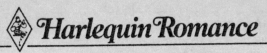

◆ Harlequin Romance

Coming Next Month

2833 SOFTLY FLITS A SHADOW Elizabeth Duke
Jilted! A broken-hearted American embarks on her honeymoon
cruise alone and attracts the attention of a fellow passenger,
who assumes she's out to catch a husband. After what she's
been through?

2834 TEMPEST IN THE TROPICS Roumelia Lane
The same meddling forestry man who's threatening her
father's Guyanese timber plantation tries to stand in the way of
a fiery daughter's plan to marry the one man she thinks could
ensure her father's future.

2835 LOVE BY DEGREE Debbie Macomber
To make ends meet when she returns to university, a mature
student plays housemother to three lovable Washington college
boys. But instead of encouragement she gets the third degree
from the owner of their cozy home.

2836 THE NIGHT IS DARK Joanna Mansell
Never get emotionally involved with clients—it's the number
one rule for Haversham girls. But an assignment in East Africa
with wildlife adventure writer Kyle Allander proved that love
makes its own rules!

2837 THE APOLLO MAN Jean S. MacLeod
Still bitter over her childhood sweetheart's sudden departure
from the Isle of Cyprus six years ago, a young islander is
suspicious of his reasons for returning . . . wary of her memories
of love.

2838 THE HARLEQUIN HERO Dixie McKeone
A romance novel fan adopts her favorite heroin's sophisticated
image to attract a living breathing hero. But her plan backfires
when he takes a page from the same book to woo the woman of
his dreams—another woman!

Available in May wherever paperback books are sold, or
through Harlequin Reader Service.

In the U.S.
901 Fuhrmann Blvd.
P.O. Box 1397
Buffalo, N.Y. 14240-1397

In Canada
P.O. Box 603
Fort Erie, Ontario
L2A 5X3

**For the millions who can't read
Give the Gift of Literacy**

One out of five adults in North America
cannot read or write well enough
to fill out a job application
or understand the directions on a bottle of medicine.

**You can change all this by joining the fight
against illiteracy.**

For more information write to:
Contact, Box 81826, Lincoln, Neb. 68501
In the United States, call toll free: 800-228-3225

**The only degree you need
is a degree of caring**

"This ad made possible with the cooperation of the Coalition for Literacy and the Ad Council."
Give the Gift of Literacy Campaign is a project of the book and periodical industry,
in partnership with Telephone Pioneers of America.

LIT—A—1

What the press says about Harlequin romance fiction...

"When it comes to romantic novels...
Harlequin is the indisputable king."
— *New York Times*

"...always with an upbeat, happy ending."
— *San Francisco Chronicle*

"Women have come to trust these
stories about contemporary people,
set in exciting foreign places."
— *Best Sellers*, New York

"The most popular reading matter of
American women today."
— *Detroit News*

"...a work of art."
— *Globe & Mail*, Toronto

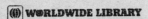

New This spring
Harlequin Category Romance Specials!
New Mix

4 Regencies—for more wit, tradition, etiquette... and romance

2 Gothics—for more suspense, drama, adventure... and romance

Regencies

***A Hint of Scandal* by Alberta Sinclair**
She was forced to accept his offer of marriage, but could she live with her decision?

***The Primrose Path* by Jean Reece**
She was determined to ruin his reputation and came close to destroying her own!

***Dame Fortune's Fancy* by Phyllis Taylor Pianka**
She knew her dream of love could not survive the barrier of his family tradition....

***The Winter Picnic* by Dixie McKeone**
All the signs indicated they were a mismatched couple, yet she could not ignore her heart's request....

Gothics

***Mirage on the Amazon* by Mary Kistler**
Her sense of foreboding did not prepare her for what lay in waiting at journey's end....

***Island of Mystery* by Margaret M. Scariano**
It was the perfect summer job, or so she thought—until it became a nightmare of danger and intrigue.

Don't miss any of them!

BPA-CAT87-1